SCATTERED

A NOVEL

Catherine Khaperska

An Imprint of Sulis International Press
Los Angeles | Dallas | London

SCATTERED: A NOVEL
Copyright 2024 by Catherine Khaperska. All rights reserved.

ISBN (print): 978-1-958139-37-0
ISBN (eBook): 978-1-958139-38-7

Published by Riversong Books
An Imprint of Sulis International
Los Angeles | Dallas | London

www.sulisinternational.com

CONTENTS

Part 1: Comet

Part 2: Scar

Part 3: Comet

To my Mom and Dad, my biggest supporters from day one. I love you both so much.

PART 1: COMET

CHAPTER 1: PUPPIES AT THE DEN

It's been hot for a couple of weeks, and it looks like it'll be hot for a couple more. I'm sick of it. So is Brescia. You see, Brescia gave birth to pups two months ago, mid-spring. Being pregnant is hard—not that I know, personally, but Brescia's told me many times. And taking care of pups in the blistering heat of the summer has got to be some sort of nightmare.

One of the pups, Ellie, saunters over with her brother, Dusty, and their other sister, Tina. They each cling to one of my legs and stare up at me adoringly. Apparently, I'm the best thing since rabbit meat and the catfish in Fog Lake.

"Hi Comet!" says Ellie excitedly, her tail wagging and her tongue hanging out of her mouth. Dusty is a little less… wild… than Ellie, but he's still really cute, and he's always happy to see me.

Dusty was born dead at first, but after a few minutes, he took his first breath. Brescia cried after she learnt Dusty wasn't breathing. She cried after he came to life, too.

Tina is the 'mature older sister', though they're practically all born at the same time. Tina just happened to come out first.

"Hey Ellie, Dusty, Tina," I say. Ellie's fur tickles my legs as she clings to them. "What brings you guys here?" Normally, they stay with either Scar or Brescia, but sometimes I get to watch them if our parents are busy.

"Mom's taking the Den to the lake for a swim!" Tina says excitedly. "Mom said we can learn to swim today, too!" I can't help smiling. They're always excited to learn new things or to meet new dogs. Swimming happens to be the thing they're learning today. Seems like only a couple of days ago they were born and did nothing but sleep. Now they're learning to swim.

"Wanna come?" Dusty says. Well, *of course* I'm coming! The whole Den is, and it's scorching outside.

"Sure, Dusty," I tell him. The three pups beam with excitement. I follow them to the lake, where they throw themselves onto Scar, who is talking to a dog named Wally. Wally came about a year ago, and he's a dachshund—what uneducated humans call 'weiner dogs' because they have elongated bodies like sausages. Wally told me that himself. I thought it was hilarious. We've even given him a nickname because of it.

"Hey, Hotdog," Darrell says as he saunters over, referring to Wally. "Hey Comet, pups." We all roll our eyes at his joke, but the pups crack up every time. Darrell's one of the older dogs at the Den—older than Brescia, even—but he doesn't resent her being his superior. I've always respected him for that. He also loves the pups—probably more than he's ever loved anyone in his life.

I walk away from the group and slip into the cool water. Someone from behind me splashes water at me and I jump. I turn to see M, our resident poodle, howling with laughter at my expression, but that turns into shrieking as I splash her back.

"I should've known," I say with a smirk. M snorts.

The pups come paddling over, just a few paces ahead of Scar. Brescia walks right beside him, and her fur fans out and floats on the surface of Fog Lake. I am suddenly taken back to another scene about two years ago, when Brescia had to have a bath at the local shelter. I bite my tongue to keep from laughing.

"So, how are the swimming lessons going?" I ask calmly. M's head flicks back and forth, watching me, then Brescia, then Scar and the pups.

"What swimming lessons?"

"We're gonna learn to swim, Auntie M!" squeals Tina. Yes, to the pups, almost everyone is a relative of some sort, either by blood or not. M and Trey are referred to as "Auntie" and they are over the moon about it. Darrell is "Uncle", even though he could be their grandfather because he's older than both Scar and Brescia.

M and I lead the pups into the shallows. The pups shriek with joy as they wade in, and the cold water gets on their sun-warmed skin. We teach them how to paddle their paws to stay afloat, and M even shows us a cool trick where you take a big breath of air, then curl up into a ball and float like a buoy. That's a ball of plastic that humans put in the water. The more I learn about humans, the stranger they are.

Tina seems to be doing well. She swims circles around her mom, making me laugh and putting a rare proud smile on Brescia's face. Ellie is happy enough flopping around where she can touch, which is funny to watch until a cold splatter of water gets in my fur. I shriek, making Ellie laugh so hard that she staggers around and splashes into Scar. Dusty is floating around, complaining about Ellie splashing, but at the same time he's quite chill. One of the qualities I love most about Dusty is that he's chill. At the Den you don't get much "chill" since there's always either something going on or Ellie's making a racket—which, for the record, I don't mind.

"Watch me! Watch me!" Ellie yells until all eyes are on her. Then she does a little flip underwater, holding her breath as her head goes under, her little fluffy ears brushing the small rocks that litter the ground. We all praise her and try it ourselves, even Darrell.

Soon the night creeps in, and the pups start shivering as the temperature drops. Brescia notices this, and calls all the dogs to get out of the water and start heading home. I join the group, and a very tired Ellie drags her paws as she follows me.

On our way back to the Den, we notice a man holding a glass bottle filled with a light-brown liquid. He's not walking straight, and he's mumbling incoherently to himself.

"Maybe we should sneak around him, he doesn't look very friendly," M says, but as soon as the sentence leaves her mouth, he spots us. His eyes take a bit of time to focus on us, and I realise suddenly that he knows we're here. Brescia gathers the pups and shoos them away, and I stay a little behind to make sure the rest of the Den is away to safety. He's a good distance away from us, but there are some leafy green plants obscuring us from view. How does he see us?

"RUDDY DOGS!" he screams, and throws his glass bottle with surprising accuracy. I turn and run a couple of metres away, and I can hear the glass shatter on a nearby rock. He also takes a small box out of his pocket as well as a lighter, and begins to smoke. Charlie never smoked, I remember, but some of his "friends" did. I can see the embers on the end of the cigarette and wonder how he can possibly smoke when it's already so hot outside. Wouldn't that be so uncomfortable? I start to smell the smoke, and suddenly, it's hard to breathe. I cough a couple of times and jog away, my friends following me.

Once we get back to the Den, we sit down at the entrance and dry up in the warm summer evening. I walk over to the pups, who are happily snuggling up against Scar. He's telling them a story I've heard a bunch of times: one about Snuffie (one of his old favourite stuffed animals) and a dinosaur. It's a good story, nonetheless, and I find myself laying down to hear it. As I listen, I'm taken back into a prehistoric world, full of huge creatures and huge plants. I shiver slightly as Scar explains how he was taken by a pterodactyl and carried into the big blue sky above.

"Scar never fails to make me happy," says a voice behind me. "His stories should be in books." I look behind me to find Brescia laying there, listening to Scar. I nod in agreement and lie against her. Ever since the pups were born, you can see the strain that they give her. Her eyes get bloodshot and puffy when she loses sleep over them. In early summer, when food was scarce and Brescia had no milk to feed them, sometimes she had to give them her food mushed up, and she'd eat from mine or Scar's hoard. This was dangerous, but necessary. Her logic was that the pups had to be fed at whatever cost, and once Brescia gets something in her head, it's very hard to change her mind.

Books are a human thing Scar told us about. Apparently, Jack used to read books to Scar, a long time ago – even ones with dinosaurs in them. Soon, with food in my tummy and leaning against Brescia's warm, strong body, my eyelids begin to get heavy. The last thing I hear before falling into a dream is something about Snuffie getting trapped in a volcano…

I don't remember the first time I felt truly safe since leaving Charlie's.

Maybe it was when I got to know Scar, that time running in the snowy woods after he tried to teach me how to hunt a squirrel. Maybe it was when I got to the shelter, and could have square meals and friends that didn't treat me like a plaything or a punching bag. Maybe it was when I got to the Den for the first time, and saw a place where I could live freely among dogs like me.

Whatever the case, there's one memory that really stands out to me. It was the evening after Scar, Brescia and I had officially become a family. Scar, on night watch duty, had decided to bring us to the edge of Foggy Lake to watch the sunrise together. It was cold lying there on the snow, but being surrounded by those I loved made it bearable.

"I love you. Both of you." Brescia had said in her rich voice, slow from sleep not yet shaken, but filled with meaning.

"Ew!" I had replied, jokingly, of course. I loved my new parents and, in that moment, would have gone to the ends of the world if it meant that I could stay with them forever.

Scar had licked the side of my face, surprising me, and then the three of us had settled comfortably on the shoreline with stupid grins on our faces.

We started a tradition from that day. Every winter since, after a snowstorm, we'd go to Foggy Lake and sit together at the water's edge, watching the sunrise turn the sky the most beautiful colours.

A reminder of what we had gone through, and how it allowed us to find each other at times when, just maybe, we needed each other most.

"There's a storm coming in a few days," Scar tells me as we're both on watch one night in early spring. At least, it should be spring. It seems like winter has lasted way longer than any winter has lasted before. He looks at me with a twinkle in his eye. "You know what that means."

"I can't wait! Brescia's been so busy with the pups that when that last storm came, we had to skip the sunrise. I hated that."

Scar looks down at the ground, a little twinge of guilt showing on his face.

"Yeah, sorry about that, love. You know how it can be with young pups. Believe me, neither Brescia nor I wanted to skip it either, but we

couldn't just leave them alone with the other Den members. Not just yet."

I nod in understanding. It had been a particularly brutal storm, with rain and snow mixed together. It had started way earlier than any of us had predicted, and the pups, along with Brescia, had gotten caught in the rain before making it home to the Den. The pups had all gotten a cold, forcing Brescia and Scar to stay home and take care of them. It had been a stressful while as Trey and I took over Alpha duties.

"But this time around, we'll go, and it'll be like old times," I say, playfully nudging Scar. "Trey or M or Darrell can watch the pups, and we can go and relax, and play around in the snow…"

"Actually, Comet, your mom and I were thinking of bringing the pups with us." Scar looks up at me hopefully, but his face falls as I gasp in shock and mild hurt. I go back to my post on the other side of the Den doorway.

"What?" he asks.

"It was our special tradition! Why would we bring the pups? It won't mean the same to them."

"They're family too, Comet. You can't discount them just because they weren't alive when you were."

I let out a humph of disappointment before realising that he's right. Scar chuckles under his breath.

"I promise, Brescia and I will make sure that it'll still be a special moment. Look at me."

I do, suppressing the urge to roll my eyes.

"We'll make sure the pups understand that this moment is important for us, and our family, alright? They're good pups, and they love you so, so much. I'm sure it'll be fine."

My expression softens and I look downwards. Scar's guilt seems to have transferred itself to me.

"I love them too, Dad. They're my siblings. But they're so young, and…" I let out a sigh. "I guess I can give them a chance."

Scar approaches me and presses his forehead to mine.

"That's my girl. And don't worry. We may have the young ones sleeping in the Den, but I never want you to feel like you aren't as important as your siblings."

Someone behind us clears their throat.

"It's my turn on watch, you guys."

Scar steps away from me and nods. As he reveals Trey behind him, I can't help but notice her contagious smile, and I grin right back.

"Have fun, Trey," I tell her.

"I'll do my best," she replies with a sigh. "By the way, Comet, the pups are asking for you. Something about your fur being cozy."

I immediately regret being angry about the idea of them at the sunrise.

"On my way."

I enter the Den and the pups are watching the door. Once they see me, they get up, tumbling over themselves, Brescia, and each other. Brescia tries to get them to sit down, then sighs and shakes her head as the pups make their way to wind around my forelegs.

"Bedtime, Comet," announces Ellie.

"I'm coming, I'm coming," I whisper. "Run to Mom, I can't move with you guys bunching around me."

The pups obey and dart over to Brescia, who smiles gratefully as I go lay down beside her. Scar, who has followed me inside, goes to plant a quick kiss on Brescia's and the pups' foreheads before curling up with his wife.

Once I'm comfortable, the pups clamber over to me and go lay down around me, closing their eyes and yawning. I watch them in awe.

"They really love you, Comet," whispers Brescia. "They look up to you."

I feel my ears get hot, then I wrap my tail around the little ones before laying my head on my paws and falling asleep myself.

My dream warps and it's a few days later, the night after the storm. It's not ridiculously bright, but I know it will be once the sun reflects off the snow-crusted ground. Brescia, Scar and I sit at the edge of Foggy Lake, with the pups between their parents, huddling for warmth.

"Two years ago, at a time just like this, I wanted to show your mom and Comet just how much I loved them," Scar murmurs to the pups. They're hanging onto his every word. "So I woke them up really early, like I did today, and I took them here to see something very special. And for you to see the really special something, you have to be paying attention, and you have to be quiet, okay?"

The pups erupt in choruses of agreement, and I can't help giggling as Brescia starts affectionately shushing them.

"Is it soon?" asks Ellie, practically vibrating from excitement.

"Very soon, sweetheart," says Brescia.

"Let's play a little game while we wait," I suggest. "I'll say I spy with my doggy eye, and then you'll guess what it is that I see. How does that sound?"

The pups all nod simultaneously, crawling around Brescia to get closer to me.

"I spy with my doggy eye... something grey."

"Rock!" starts Dusty.

"That rock!" exclaims Ellie.

"Dad?" guesses Tina.

"Correct! It was Dad," I reply. "Nice job."

Tina beams with pride, and I can't help the warm feeling spreading through my body, from the tips of my ears to the end of my fluffy husky tail.

"I spy with my doggy eye the special something," announces Brescia, and the pups run back to where they were sitting as I turn around to face the lake. The sunrise, full of oranges and pinks and purples, impresses the pups so much that for once, they're completely speechless.

"It's pretty!" cries Dusty. "And you get to see this every year?"

"Every day, if we wanted to," says Brescia, and the pups gasp and turn to look at her in awe.

"Every day?"

"We only do this after storms though because it's a special time for Comet, your father, and I," says Brescia.

"Okay!" says Ellie. "Can we come next time too?"

I decide to answer before anyone else can beat me to it.

"Of course. You – and Dusty and Tina – are part of our family. We would never leave you out."

Scar gives me a proud smile. It's in that moment when I remember just how much I love this family. Not just my parents, who I've known for years, but also my new beautiful siblings. I'm their older sister, and I'll do anything to make sure they know they're loved and safe. I can't wait to see what happens in the future.

I wake up rather unfortunately to a loud huff from M. I open one eye and look around, wondering what's going on.

"Oh – sorry, Comet. The pups just got to sleep, and the stars are starting to disappear, which means I don't have much time before they wake up again. And I bet they're not even going to be tired tomorrow! How do they do it?" M complains in an angry whisper, plopping down next to me. I sigh affectionately as I look at my siblings, whose chests rise and fall easily. I can tell Ellie's having a good dream, since she kicks her legs around sometimes as if she's trying to run.

"They're very energetic, that's for sure. You should go to sleep now, though. Your eyes can barely stay open long enough to look at me." This gets a tired laugh out of M, and she lays down and closes her eyes. In seconds, her breath comes evenly and I can tell she's asleep.

Ellie kicks out once, and smacks Tina by accident. She rolls over, muttering uncomfortably, but I don't think she's woken up. I lay back down and close my eyes, sleep taking over me once again.

CHAPTER 2: THE FIRE

"Fire!" screams Brescia, bursting in the Den. I'm still a bit tired, but by the angle of the sun coming through the window of the Den, it's about five in the morning. I'm groggy and still only half-awake.

"What…?" I begin, then I yawn.

"Comet, we need to go!" says Brescia urgently. "We have to evacuate, get everyone out of the Den, now!" I jump up immediately.

"Why?" I ask, almost drifting off again.

"Fire!" yells Scar from outside. "Everyone, get to the street corner over there! We need to get as far away as possible! Run! Now!"

Adrenaline bursts through my veins as I leap to my paws and begin rousing dogs.

"THE PUPS!" I yelp. "Where are they?"

"Pups, to me!" Brescia screams. In the rush of dogs, I can somewhat see small dogs running to Brescia, but I can't tell exactly who they are. I hope that all the pups have found their mom, but at this point, Brescia's got that situation handled, and I have to help the rest of the Den. I don't know how much time we have left.

I go around, rousing dogs from sleep and telling them to run, go find Scar at the street corner, evacuate as fast as possible. Most of them listen to me, some take a bit more persuasion. I suppose the urgency in my voice is what does it. I see Trey rousing M, and Brescia crying out to Darrell

(*Leave your stuff, you don't need it! Go find Scar!*) and I see the pups' scared expressions as the crackling coming from the fire in the forest gets louder.

"We have to go! Everyone out!" I call. I hear younger dogs wailing and older dogs grumbling. Most of us are in a mass panic. I run around making sure everyone gets out safely. Suddenly, I hear a small, plaintive voice call from the Den.

"Comet?! Mom!?"

I turn so fast I almost crack my neck and see Ellie, frozen in shock. She must not have followed Brescia out of the Den, scared out of her mind. I turn and run back.

"Comet, what are you doing!" yells Trey. "Come on!"

"Brescia's pup—*my sister*—is still stuck in the Den!" I yell back. I turn without waiting for Trey's response as I run back towards the Den and grab Ellie by the scruff of the neck. Ellie's small body trembles as I carry her back to Brescia, who's terrified expression changes to relief within seconds. I notice Trey running back to the Den, and I catch up with her.

"Trey, what are you doing?" I ask her. "There's no one left in the Den, come on, we have to go!" She looks back at me and then at the Den. Then back at me again.

"Just one last time, let's check that the Den's really and truly empty," Trey says, then runs back into the Den. I'm hesitant, since the fire looks awfully close to the Den (some parts of it are already starting to smoke and get warm), but if there is still a chance to save someone, I'd rather go help than not, and lose someone.

I find Trey coaxing an older dog to run, to go save herself. The older dog is frightened to the point of tears, and won't get out of the corner, saying "if I die, I die, I can't leave... my only home—my home..." Trey is grabbing her paw and speaking gently, but still, the dog won't leave. I notice there are a few other scared dogs in the area too. I wonder how we missed them the first time around. Maybe we didn't, they just refused to leave when we asked them to.

"COME ON!" I yell over the crackling of the fire, slowly getting louder. Trey helps the old dog up, and we start running. The rest of the dogs from the Den are in front, I'm in the middle, and Trey, with the old dog on our heels, is bringing up the rear.

I chance a look outside the Den windows. The glass, starting to fog up from the smoke, shows that the uncut, unkempt dry grass surrounding the Den is on fire, and slowly spreading. There isn't nearly enough time, but we're all driven by the same hope, whether or not it is a futile one. I wish I could run as fast as my legs can take me, but I can't leave Trey behind with the older dog, who's much slower than the rest (as expected).

"Can we go any faster?" I ask, whipping my head around to look behind and ahead of me at the same time.

"We're trying," says Trey, disgruntled. The old dog puts on a small burst of speed upon seeing that the walls of the Den are starting to catch on fire. It suddenly gets much, *much* hotter. The old dog, fueled by panic and adrenaline, bursts ahead of me, and I follow her out. I hear yelps behind me and see that the ceiling is collapsing, delaying Trey and forcing her to jump over flaming shingles and wooden planks.

"I got it, it's okay. I'm right behind you," says Trey. "Stupid fire." I nod. The rest of the way out of the Den looks clear enough. As I go on, I hear crackling and crashing behind me.

Finally, I run through the yet-unburnt grass to the street, where I'm safe. I turn around, wondering where Trey is, when I see that my exit to the Den has been caved in.

Trey is still inside.

I want to run towards her. I want to pull the flaming wood away from the exit. Logically, I know that I'll just end up burnt too, if only my paws. In the rush, though, I don't care. I don't care if my paws get burned, if my best friend ends up making it out alive.

"COMET, NO!" yells Scar. "LOOK!" The next few events happen within seconds.

I look at Scar. I follow his gaze. I see a flaming tree from the forest begin to tip over. I notice its trajectory going straight over the Den. There's no time to scream, shout, or cry anything comprehensible, and the only sound I can make is a vague choking sound as I'm frozen in place, this huge tree slowly falling.

It lands with a crash right on top of the Den, engulfing it in flame.

"NO!" I scream, as I understand what just happened. Trey didn't make it out of the Den in time. She used her last strength and sacrificed her life to save one old dog, frozen with shock and refusing to leave. She helped her and made sure she got out safe, and it cost her everything. And what did I do? I ran. Like a coward.

"TREY!" I shriek. "NO!"

I understand that there's no way to save my best friend anymore, but my body somehow forces me to run towards her, towards the Den. Scar grabs onto me and digs his teeth so hard into me that it hurts. But that pain is nothing compared to the pain of knowing that Trey is gone, or will be gone, very soon.

"Comet, stop," I hear Scar say, his voice monotone. "It's too dangerous."

"TREY!! NO!!" I yell. I don't think I've yelled so hard in my life. I can't even yell anything else, just Trey's name, repeating over and over in my head.

"Comet, face it, she's… she was a hero. You did your best, damn it, we all did our best but sometimes… sometimes…" Scar says, a sob escaping his mouth, his voice brittle, broken. I'm so stunned by his tone that I stop struggling. Scar doesn't cry, he doesn't. But there he is.

I look at the Den burning, consumed by fire and ashes and smoke. There is no way Trey made it out alive. I go completely limp as Scar holds me. I see the Den for what is probably the last time, and I notice firefighters hosing down the Den with water, but deep down I know it's no use.

I'm still alive.

My family is alive.

But Trey is dead. She's gone.

It hurts to think of it so literally. The word 'gone' seems softer, but 'gone' implies that she can be found.

Let's face it. She's dead, and she's not coming back.

I am vaguely aware of the humans moving in on the Den, spraying it down with more and more water as the fire continues to rage across the field in front of us.

My only home, destroyed. Suddenly, I can't breathe. The floor seems to zoom in and out, and I can't see Scar anymore, though I swear he was right beside me. Scar feels the change, and drops me in surprise. I stagger, shocked.

Trey. The Den.

My sister. My home.

Gone.

I wake up, groan and open my eyes. I smell smoke in the air, and wonder what's going on. Is the Den having a campfire? That's a human thing where they burn wood, but I don't know how dogs could have started one. I get up, and wobble a bit. *Why am I outside?*

"Whoa, Comet. Maybe you should lay down for a bit," Scar's voice says from behind me. A surge of adrenaline rushes through me as all of the previous night's activities demand to be recognized. I look around, making sure my memories are not a dream. There are dogs scattered on the ground, sleeping. We're in an alleyway somewhere in the city, twenty or so dogs, crammed into one place. My stomach boils, and I quickly sidestep Scar to get to the end of the alley. Much better.

"Where... where are we?" I ask, my voice trembling a bit. I certainly don't remember being in this part of the city.

"We're actually only a couple of kilometres from Jack's and the dog park," Scar tells me. "This alleyway was where I found you all those years ago." I shudder a little, remembering Scar's story.

"Why here?" I ask. "Why not any other alleyway?" Scar shrugs.

"It was the only alleyway I could think of which had enough scraps to feed all of us, since our food got burnt up along with the rest of the Den."

And Trey.

My throat seizes up, and I find it hard to breathe, but I stop myself. I will *not* cry here. I clear my throat and face Scar again, with a smile that seems forced, even to me.

"Well, it's definitely spacious," I say sarcastically, giving the place a dirty look. Scar gives a small smile that quickly fades.

"Well, we don't want to get caught, and this is somewhere almost no one goes, and it's nicely sheltered." Caught. Right. Stupid me. We can't have this many dogs running around Fog Lake City.

"You should get some sleep," Scar says, giving me a sideways look, probably trying to figure out if I'm going to start crying uncontrollably again or something.

"Sleep?" I ask, my voice a bit hoarse. "You think I can sleep at a time like this? And I don't mean the fact that the sun isn't even close to setting." Besides, I *was* just unconscious for goodness knows how long.

"You'll be fine," Scar says simply. I look into his eyes, looking for something, anything. Support, sadness, anything that shows he's been affected by what's just happened, and that I'm not alone in whatever roller-coaster is going on in my mind. Scar's gotten better at masking his emotions, though. I don't see anything that suggests he is grieving, and yet I know he is. I lay down and pretend to close my eyes, waiting.

Nothing happens for about thirty minutes. But then, as I'm starting to get tired, I see Scar's body tremble with the sobs he is refusing to let out. I get up and stare at Scar. I haven't seen him cry in a long, *long* time. I see Brescia get up and put her paw on his back, and he looks up at her with an expression that says, "what do we do now?" I lay down slowly, but it takes me a long time before I can calm down enough to sleep.

CHAPTER 3: MISTRUST AND MISERY

I wake up to a searing hot pain on my back. I jump up, panic rushing through my veins again, only to see it's because the sun is up. I've been sleeping in the sun for what was probably about an hour. The alleyway is emptier than before. I suppose some dogs have gone in search of food. My stomach grumbles, and I realise I haven't had food in a while. M is sitting alone at the very back of the alleyway. She doesn't move as I go to sit next to her. Both of us stare at the dirty wall, deep in thought.

"COMET!" Ellie's voice shrieks from behind me. I turn to see a very excited Ellie with a burrito in her mouth.

"I caught something! I don't really know what it is. But I still caught it!" she says, wearing a proud look of accomplishment. I snort.

"Ellie, that's a burrito, and a half-eaten one at that," I tell her. She looks confused.

"What's a burtito?" she asks. "Is it eatable?"

M and I burst out laughing. Soon we are rolling around over the warm cement, howling with laughter. It seems so wrong to be laughing, but that thought just makes me laugh even harder. We've been stressed for so long, that this laughing sort of helps let go, in a way. We're probably laughing way too hard, but we can't keep it in anymore. I'm afraid that if I stop laughing, I'll never laugh again. A burrito! Is a burrito eatable? *Eatable?*

I try to stop, but one look at Ellie's curious face, and it sets me off again. Finally, I stop, and M stops shortly afterward. I grin.

"It's pronounced *burrito*, and yes, it's edible, Ellie," I say between hiccups. The sound of my hiccups almost set me off again, but then I see that the whole Den is staring at me.

"Comet, is everything—are you okay?" asks Brescia.

"I'm fine." I try to compose myself, but then I start giggling. After a couple more minutes, I finally calm down. I look Brescia in the eye and ask her if anything new happened while I was gone. She sighs and flops down onto the ground.

"No. Nothing," she says. "We found a stash of food that we're working hard to bring back here. We do need a proper place to live, though."

"You can say that again," says Scar from behind her, his mouth full of a couple of bones, probably from a family having steak ribs.

Scar drops the bones in the back of the alleyway and comes over to nuzzle Brescia with his nose. She sighs, and the tension in her body from stress loosens, and she nuzzles him back. They're so cute together that it makes my heart ache.

"Comet, why don't you go follow Scar and help us get the food over here?" asks Brescia. "We have a lot of mouths to feed tonight, and we have practically no food, unlike…" *Unlike back at the Den, where we had a good life and a good home.* I nod frantically to hide the shaking in my limbs.

The day goes on slowly, and I can feel the restlessness in the air. I don't know if it's the painful memories of what happened before, the discomfort of the now, or the worry for the future, but even the pups have mellowed down and are looking at everyone warily. The mood is definitely lower, and any time you make eye contact with anyone, you see either sadness or anger.

Darrell soon gets hungry and grabs some food from the mini-hoard that we had managed to compile, and apparently a Dalmatian wanted that same bit of food. From what I know and what little I've been told about Darrell's backstory, he used to be a fighter, so this could have been a really bad situation. Darrell chooses to just give up the food he picked to reduce the conflict. I go to check on him to see if he's okay, and he waves me off with a small smile.

"I can always get more food," he says. "Don't wanna make things worse."

It feels like everyone's a time bomb of some sort, just waiting for the right thing to set them off. I don't know what it is, but everyone can feel it.

Some time later, I decide to follow Scar to the alleyway with the food. Better to be productive than sit around wasting time and worrying. It's a couple of blocks away, but with all the people and everything, the streets are packed. No wonder it's taking so long for everyone to get the food back to where we're hanging out. I grab what looks like a bag with a two-thirds-eaten burger, and Scar takes a bag with a couple of bites worth of hot-dog, and we head back to the alleyway where Brescia's waiting with Tina and Dusty. The pups attack the hotdog like they'll never eat again, and I snort with laughter. They're practically on top of one another.

Scar, a few other members of the Den and I transfer food to the alleyway for a few hours, and soon we have a large enough heap of food for the time being. We all sit around, eating and chatting. Suddenly, I sit up straight and listen. I'm sure I hear my name being called, or a muffled call. I turn towards the entrance of the alleyway and see a rather strange sight.

Ellie runs towards us with another leftover burrito half shoved in her mouth. She plops it down in front of everyone and starts complaining about how her mouth hurts. Brescia laughs and walks up to her, picking her up by the scruff of her neck and setting her down next to her siblings.

"Shouldn't have put such a big burrito in your mouth, you silly goose," teases Scar. He takes it and shares it between the three pups and himself. Everyone eats, not just burritos, but also most of the food we got from the neighbouring alleyway. I don't know if everyone's had enough, but I sure hope so. We're gonna have to find more food if we're gonna get everyone fed tomorrow. We've got a lot of work cut out for us.

I lay down, right at the alleyway entrance, feeling the warm summer air on my back and watching the pups play "Crawl Over Scar". It's funny to watch, but at the same time, Scar is getting prodded and poked by twelve puppy legs, and it's probably not very comfortable.

I approach Brescia as the cool afternoon turns into an even cooler evening. She's talking with another group of dogs, and they look angry, while Brescia looks defeated. I probably should be more shocked, but she's been dealing with a lot of angry dogs, amidst her own grief and her pups. I don't think she has the strength to keep up a facade anymore.

"What's going on, Mom?" I ask. Brescia gives me a weak smile as the group of dogs turns to me with all sorts of negative emotions flashing in their eyes.

"I'll tell you what's going on," snarls the head of this group, a tall Dalmatian (the same one from earlier). He stares Brescia directly in the eyes. "Our home is gone, our food is dwindling, and we're no longer out of the public eye. You trusted Scar to find us a place, and look where we are. Look what we've reduced ourselves to!" Brescia raises her eyebrows, doing her best to keep neutral, but I can tell by the flicking of her tail that they've unsettled her.

"I'm sorry you feel this way, truly," she says softly. "I had no control over the situation. We're doing the best we can. If you're hungry, we have food… if there's anything else you need, please let me know, and we'll figure out a solution together, like we always have."

"Are you trying to start some sort of rebellion or something?" I ask the Dalmatian, my eyes looking to the other dogs behind him as well. "We'll find a home soon enough, we just gotta work together." Brescia shoots me a glance and I go quiet. The dogs in the group snarl, rolling their eyes and looking at each other. I think they see how nervous Brescia is, and a nervous, defensive Brescia is almost as scary as an angry one.

"We'll get some food, if you'll allow us to," says their designated leader sarcastically, and Bresica nods meekly. "But this isn't over."

Brescia just keeps nodding, letting them pass her on their way to the food. One of them makes an effort to sneer at her, another bumps into her so she staggers, almost knocking me over. She regains her footing and shakes her head. I wonder how she manages to keep herself together. I'd have broken down by now.

"I'm alright, Comet, you don't have to worry about me," she tells me in a low voice. "At least *you* still trust me, right?"

"Of course I do, you're my mom! You've never let me down before, of course I trust you!"

"Everyone's stressed. They want to know what our next steps are, that's the big question on everyone's mind, and for once, I can't tell them." Her voice breaks. "I'm just hoping they can still trust me."

"They trusted you this far," I tell her. "I'm sure they can still find it in them to trust you. After all, you're the reason they're alive, if you think about it." Brescia just sighs again and nods. The topic of the one who isn't sits untouched between us.

"I suppose so. But for once in my life I'm not this paragon of leadership, and everything falls apart. I just wish we could roll back time."

"If there are dogs who want to leave the Den, that's their problem, not yours. The Den gave them everything, and they shouldn't throw it away because something went wrong." Despite these words, I can feel why Brescia's worried. Even if it's just one thing that went wrong, you gotta admit the wrong here is very, *very* wrong.

"You're right. We'll figure things out, in the end." She takes a deep, grounding breath. She takes a few seconds to pull herself up and put on the leadership facade. I don't reply, just smile and trot off to find M. As much as I probably should want to be alone, I can't find it in myself to leave the alleyway without a friend by my side.

When night falls, and everyone starts settling in, Ellie suddenly jumps up and starts running around, barking her head off at a dark shape with two big lights in the distance. I sit up straight and try to make out the blobs of light coming towards us.

"RUN!" Brescia screams as we see a truck pull up beside the alleyway with the shelter logo on the side. It looks like a dog, but the head is shaped like an upside-down heart with two ears.

Three humans hop out of the truck and run towards us. They hold tranquiliser guns and have thick gloves and gear on, even though it's so hot out. Theories run through my mind, but after only a few seconds, it's clear. Someone must have seen us in the alleyway and called the shelter. That's the only explanation for why they're so prepared. We're all tired and well-fed, so it's hard for many of us to get moving fast.

The humans grab as many dogs as possible, putting them in the back of the truck in small metal cages. Just the thought of being in one of those things again makes me start trembling like a leaf. One after another, dogs are being snatched from the streets and put in the truck. I run towards Brescia, who has Dusty and Tina with her, but Ellie is nowhere to be seen. She was the closest dog to the humans, so I have no idea where she is now. She might as well be in the man's truck already. As I run, I get this nauseating feeling that someone is right behind me. I look back and see a man's hands reaching out to grab me. I put on a burst of speed and make it to Brescia, almost falling down in the process. Brescia bares her teeth and snarls at the men, who are careful but still inching closer. Scar arrives and starts barking and growling so intensely that I'm surprised the men aren't running away.

The man turns around and starts snatching other dogs. I see M struggling in the arms of the man with the tranq. I see Darrell, limp in the arms of another. Another dog, locked in the cage in the truck and howling. My ears are ringing so hard that I barely register anything else. I'm frozen in place, and my only thoughts are about staying with Scar and Brescia, and scanning for Ellie. Everyone is running farther and farther and scattering everywhere, making it easier for the humans to focus on one dog and capture them.

"Don't be stupid!" I yell. "They'll catch you if you're alone! Don't you see?" Nobody is listening to me. *Oh, for the love of kibble...*

Suddenly, I see her. One of the human figures has Ellie by the scruff of her neck. The figure looks female, and I think she's trying to comfort my wailing sister, rather unsuccessfully. The next thing I see is a blur of fur and anger as Brescia jumps on the human and bares her teeth, snarling. One of the other humans shoots a tranq dart that just misses Brescia as she jumps off of the woman.

I howl with rage, adrenaline pulsing through my veins, and grab onto the woman's arm, forcing her to drop Ellie. Scar rushes to Ellie and drags her to safety, as Brescia drags me away from the panicking dogs and the humans. We all huddle together, Scar and Brescia shielding me and the pups. Most of the Den seems to have scattered, but a few are still struggling as the shelter workers try to soothe the rampaging dogs and load them into the truck. One of the humans breaks away from the group and heads towards where Scar and Brescia are protecting me and the pups. He smells familiar, and I realise it's Mike, the worker who took care of us two years ago.

"It's okay, it's okay," he coos. Scar and Brescia back up closer to us and growl as Mike sees us behind them. A look of confusion flashes over Mike's face before he comprehends the scene. Two parents protecting their family.

"This is no place for a pup to live, out on the streets," he says. "Don't worry, little ones, I'll give you all a nice home with all the food you could want, and a lot of new friends, and maybe you'll be adopted by some nice family that will love you and care for you! How does that sound?"

That sounds horrible.

Unexpectedly, I hear frightened yelping coming from behind me.

"MAMA! DADDY! COMET! HELP!" Ellie wails as a shelter worker sets her into a cage. She bites his finger, but he's wearing gloves.

With dread, I remember that the alleyway has a back door, so to speak. There's another van parked there, blocking the way.

Brescia turns so fast I'm surprised she doesn't give herself whiplash, and mutters something under her breath that I can't hear, but Scar's eyebrows shoot up.

They have Ellie. *They have my sister!* I start running towards the shelter worker who grabbed her, but Scar barrels up and stops me from going.

"What are you doing?" I ask. "Don't you see they have her? I can do it, I can…"

"I'm not going to lose two daughters tonight," Scar says in a broken voice. "They have her, but they can't have you."

"We're not losing any daughters tonight, we're going with her," Brescia declares, "then we'll break out of the shelter before anyone can adopt one of us. We've done it before, and we'll do it again."

Brescia sits at the shelter worker's feet and starts whining. Me, Scar and the pups (those who haven't been caught yet) join her. I start howling, and all of the dogs in the various vans and trucks begin to howl too, and I hear some howlers farther away, the ones who've escaped. I put on my best puppy dog eyes and the shelter worker gives me a smile.

"Boy, there are a lot of you, aren't there?" he asks with the same smile, growing ever faker to the point of it being unsettling. I wonder if his teeth are secretly painted. There's no way anyone's teeth are reasonably that white.

Finally, he lowers a cage near Brescia, and she climbs into it without hesitation. The workers put Scar in the truck next, and I consider grabbing Tina and Dusty and making a run for it, but the look in Brescia's eyes deters me. I don't struggle (much) as the shelter worker lifts me up and sets me down in a cage and closes it. Oh, no… no… no!

"No, no, no, no, no, let me out!" I cry as I pace around in my cage. Mike stares at me for a second, then turns around to look at Scar and Brescia.

"No… it can't be," he mumbles. His eyes land on the scar crossing from Scar's left eyebrow down to the bottom of his eye. "Alright, fine, calm down." Mike opens my cage and sets me down next to Scar's cage as he puts Tina and Dusty in the truck. He closes the trunk and I hear crunching gravel as he walks to the front seat.

"It's him, I swear, and that small husky pup's grown up, and the German Shepherd we needed to give a bath to… the one with the worm stuck on her leg."

"Can't be! How could it possibly be the same dogs? Come on now, Mike," says another, the younger one with the ridiculously white teeth.

"No, no, it's them, Max, Hunter and Brownie, plus some little puppies that need naming," argues Mike.

"How do you even remember that?"

"Oh come on, you remember them too, Caleb, the ones with Maisie." Maisie. A flicker of hope rises in me. Maybe she's still at the shelter.

Then the doors close, and just before we are totally confined to the back of the truck, I can see the dogs that managed to escape. Good. Very good. I think they can figure things out by themselves, after all, they're Den members.

38

The engine starts up again. Brescia looks furious to be in human possession again but relieved that at least we're all together. Scar's face is blank, too many emotions going through him. Dusty and Tina are huddled together. Dusty is starting to whimper and Tina's comforting him, saying *at least we're with Mom, Dad, and Comet*. Ellie's trying to roll her cage closer to her siblings' cage. Every time the cage rotates onto another one of its sides, Ellie is thrown to the ground, but she seems to find it funny. As for me, all I can think about is how to calm myself down and not let my claustrophobia consume me. Then my eyes close, and despite all the events of the past day (has it really only been a day?) I fall asleep.

CHAPTER 4: A FAMILIAR SIGHT

I wake up on a smooth surface. My nose burns as the most putrid scent hits me. I raise my head, and see two people without legs. Oh, never mind, I'm just on a table.

"No fleas, she's good to go," Mike says.

"What about ticks?" the other asks. This one is unfamiliar.

"Nope, already checked." I sit up, looking around. The walls are grey, and there's a door on the far side of the room. I'm on a table with a light directly above me. Mike opens the door, and I hop down from the table. They bring me to a very familiar room with cages and food dishes.

The first thing I notice is how many dog heads turn towards me as I enter the room. I know the men checking my fur for parasites just told me I had none, but my skin seems to have tiny bugs crawling all over it.

"Um… hi?" I start cautiously. A general ambience fills the room as everyone restarts their conversations. But the awkward silence as I walked in set off alarms in my brain. Did something happen that I wasn't aware of? Are Scar and Brescia doing okay? Are the pups alright? I start to hyperventilate, and have to close my eyes to get my breathing to slow down. Last night's events have set my nerves on edge, and I don't know when they'll stop panicking.

Brescia walks up to me and I sigh. She's doing alright, at least.

"Welcome to what's going to be our home for the next little while," she says. I'd expect her to be upset about it, but at this point I bet she's just grateful to have a roof above her head and some nice food every day.

"So many new dogs here... I don't recognize anyone." My heart sinks as I say those words. Porter, Chester, and Maisie are probably all gone by now. I mean, it's not like I fully expected to see them here. It's been over two years since I last saw them.

"When you had your little checkup with Mike, I got to know the dogs here. And it's true that there are many un-familiar faces, but I do know someone who's been dying to see you again." My ears perk up at this, but before I can ask who it is, someone—a big, slim, grey, furry someone—gets up from where she had been napping and walks to-wards us, all her teeth showing in a grin.

It's Maisie.

She's fully grown, and looks nothing like the cute, fuzzy, adorable dog I met when I was just a pup. She looks lean-er and stronger, and she has teeth that would make Scar jealous. But underneath all of that, is Maisie. She still has fluffy ears, and her tongue is lolling out of her mouth.

"Maisie?" I whisper. I can't believe it. "Maisie!"

"Comet!!! Hi!! I can't believe it's really you!!"

"Unless you know another three-year-old husky, it's most definitely me." She barrels into me and gives me a huge hug. Greyhounds are rather thin, and her bony shoulder digs into mine. But I barely register the discom-fort. I didn't think I'd ever see Maisie again, but here she is, and here I am.

"Tell me everything!" I gush. "What happened? Where are the others? Were they adopted?"

"Yes, everyone except for me," Maisie pouts, "then so many new dogs came all at the same time! Your turn!

What's happened since you… OH MY GOODNESS!" Maisie squeals as the pups run over and nuzzle me. "PUPPIES!"

"These are Scar and Brescia's pups. That's Ellie," I say, licking her cheek. "Tina," I say, putting a paw on her head. "And Dusty." I gesture to him, currently trying to detach his tail from the rest of his body.

"Oh my gosh, they're so cute!" gushes Maisie. "Hi, little ones!" The pups give her a look up and down, then they crawl over to her and lay down in front of her. As if on cue, they all start doing the cutest little things, like pawing each other, nuzzling up to Maisie, and sneezing. Clearly overwhelmed, Maisie looks at me and tries not to start squealing again.

"Comet, you're so lucky," she says softly. "You have the cutest siblings ever. And a loving family. And skills that aren't simply being able to *stay*, *fetch*, and *heel*." I feel my face go hot, and I shrug.

"It's not that big of a deal," I say. Before Maisie can contradict me, Jack comes walking in with bags of food. I gobble up all my food, then lay down on the cold tile floor, my stomach heavy and my mind overwhelmed. I fall into a deep, deep sleep right then and there.

It doesn't even feel like an hour later when I wake up with a pup jumping around me, though judging by the fact that my food bowl has been refilled, it's probably the morning. I don't feel rested at all.

"SHE'S AWAKE!" Ellie shrieks as she jumps at me.

"Yes, I'm awake, you silly goose," I say while Ellie rolls over on the floor with a giggle. "Where's Mom and Dad?"

"I'm not a goose! Oh, and they're over there, talking about 'grown-up stuff'." Ellie makes air-quotes by emphasising two tail-swishes. Sure enough, Scar and Brescia are in the corner, talking in low voices and occasionally looking up. I wonder what they're talking about. I get up and shake myself, then start walking towards the corner.

I am rapidly interrupted by another four pairs of puppy paws in front of me. Dusty and Tina each grab onto a front leg and ask me to play with big excited eyes. I lick their foreheads and smile. It pains me to say no, but I have to figure out why Scar and Brescia are arguing.

"Maybe later, you guys. I just woke up." To emphasise my point, I yawn and stretch. Dusty mimics my yawn and stretch, making his sisters laugh so hard I bet their sides hurt.

I catch a bit of what Scar and Brescia are saying as I get closer.

"No, that wouldn't work—"

"You're right, they're always watching."

"What are you guys talking about?" I interrupt, gesturing for the pups to leave. They do.

"Nothing, just—" Scar begins, but Brescia cuts him off.

"She's not a pup anymore, Scar, and Comet should be more involved in what's going on around here. After all, she's almost the age you were when you found her."

Wow, I'm old. (Sorry, Scar.)

"Did something happen?" I ask.

"Scar and I were wondering how we can get out of here before, well, before one of us gets adopted," Brescia explains.

Oh. Oh, no.

She's right. Eventually, we're going to be adopted, and I highly doubt that people will want to adopt six dogs all at once. People normally want cute little puppies with cute little tails, meaning the pups would be the first to go. They're the youngest, the most trainable, adorable and irresistible of us all. There is a chance they could get adopted all together in one family, but what if they get separated? What if *I'm* the first one to get adopted, or Scar, or Brescia?

"You shouldn't have told her," Scar says in a voice that sounds like he's trying not to get angry as he takes in my expression.

"Yes, you're right, I shouldn't have told her we were planning to escape to *prevent* anyone getting adopted," Brescia counters.

"You know what I mean!"

After being here for some time, getting to know everyone and how everything runs around here after two long years of being away, people start filtering in, coming to adopt dogs. A woman dressed all in pink and with an expensive-looking purse adopts a bulldog from the Den named Sam. I haven't known him as well as anyone else, but still, it was a shock to see how *willing* he was to get adopted. He was a bit nervous at first, but once she started talking to him in a small cutesy voice, he was sold.

"Bye everyone! I'll miss you, but this lady seems cool!" He climbs in and soon gets carried out in a dog carrier. Watching him makes my skin crawl, and gives me shivers all up and down my spine. How could he *stand* being in such a small space? I watch the back of the woman's pink sequined tank top until the door closes behind her.

Scar begins pacing and grinding his teeth about a minute after Sam leaves. Brescia looks alarmed at this sudden change in him.

"Scar, what in the world is going on with you?" she asks, her ears flickering around as if she can't decide whether to go Angry Mom Mode or not.

"Sam was *just* adopted," he mutters angrily. "He won't be the only one, mark my words. I don't want these people to tear my family apart the way they've done in the past. I've done too much to keep us together, and I'm not... I can't..." Scar takes a deep breath in through his teeth, making a hissing noise. He lets it out in a growl, his ears going back.

Brescia lets out a soft 'oh', as if she had suddenly released all the air in her lungs. Scar immediately runs over to her, anger dissolved as he rushes to support and comfort his wife.

"I'm sorry, I never meant to scare you, or make you upset..."

I almost tear up. Scar worships the ground Brescia walks on. Of course, I knew this before, he's always in a better mood around her (as well as the rest of us Den members) but it seems that especially now he wants to make sure she knows he loves her. Especially now when there's a possibility he won't be able to do it later.

"I'm okay, Scar, love."

"It's not. You say it is, but it's not." Scar deflates, collapsing on the floor. "I wish... I wish we could just get out of here. Raise our kids to be free and independent. I wish we could have seen Comet meet someone, start her own family."

"Scar, darling, you say that like we have a choice," Brescia tells him. "Our kids *are* strong and independent, but just because there are humans around does not mean that those qualities they've grown to have will be gone."

"You're right, I suppose," Scar replies. "You're always right, even if I don't like how *right* you are."

Brescia chuckles.

"I know."

The next day, another visitor shows up. She's a young-ish woman, wearing a simple t-shirt and jeans shorts. She looks confident, almost overly so. She probably has experience with dogs, and more likely than not, will leave with another dog behind her. Mike, who is standing with her, looks overwhelmed and a bit intimidated. I stand near the back of the room so as to hide the pups. She can't take one of them. Not yet, not now, not ever.

"We have a bunch of new dogs here, they're not a hundred percent ready to be pets, but you're willing to familiarise yourself with them. I'm sure they won't harm you in any way," Mike tells her, then turns and closes the door behind him when he leaves.

"Hi!" says the woman, kneeling down. She looks at Maisie and begins petting her. Maisie, on her end, smiles and relaxes under this woman's touch.

"I like her," says Maisie, closing her eyes and grinning. Meanwhile, a feeling of doom is growing in my stomach.

"Maisie, no! Don't leave!" I cry out.

The woman stands up after petting Maisie and seems to see me for the first time.

"Hey, lil' husky girl. What's your name?" She doesn't look for the name on my cage, just kneels down in front of me. All the fur on my back stands on end, and my ears flatten. The pups run to their parents while all the attention from this woman is focused on me. I don't like this attention, and I don't like *her*, contrary to whatever Maisie thinks.

The woman reaches her hand out to pet me, and I snap my teeth at her. She pulls her hand back sharply, then laughs.

"No, silly, we don't bite people! Good dogs don't bite!"

Yeah, well, I guess I'm not a good dog, then. But at the moment, I don't *want* to be a good dog. I don't want to get adopted, and I'll bite anyone who tries to take me away from my family and the only home I have at the moment.

The woman reaches her hand out to pet me again, this time higher as she goes to pet my head. I raise my head and snap at her again.

"Nuh-uh-uh!" The woman tells me in a singsong voice. "What did I tell you about biting people?"

She must think I'm about Ellie's age. *I remember what you told me, I'm not stupid. And I'll keep biting you as long as you try to pet me!*

Finally, one more snap later, the woman stands up, clearly annoyed. Good.

"Bad dog! No biting!" Then she looks around for other dogs to pet and get to know. I approach Brescia and Scar as the woman moves around to some of the dogs that I never got the chance to properly get to know and befriend. Probably a good thing I didn't, though, since if I did, they'd be yet another friend of mine viciously torn out of my life. As long as everyone from the Den is safe (and Maisie, of course) that's what matters.

"Comet, I'm hungry," says Tina in a small voice once I get next to her. "When do we eat?"

I look at Scar helplessly.

"Soon, hopefully," he says. I hear a stomach rumbling, and something tells me it's Scar's.

"Comet, about you snapping and stuff…" Brescia starts. I look at her incredulously.

"Would you rather I be compliant? Allow her to pet me? What if she decided she wanted to…" My heart lodges itself in my throat as the scenario plays out in my mind. "To… take me home with her?"

Brescia sighs.

"I… you're right. I was going to say something along the lines of 'maybe you could've been a little nicer' or 'set an example for the pups' but… I can't. You did the right thing in the moment. I wouldn't want you to sacrifice us to keep up a good image for your younger siblings."

"Thanks, Mom," I reply, relieved that I'm not in trouble or anything like that. Brescia gives me a small smile, and while I should be happy about that, I know that I might never see a grin on my adoptive mother's face for a long time. Not after the fire, not after what it did to Trey.

Not here. Not soon.

I sigh and flop down on the ground. Maisie cautiously walks up to me, but keeps her distance. I see her out of the corner of my eye and I raise an eyebrow at her.

"I'm not going to bite *you*, you know. You don't have to be scared of me," I assure her. After that, Maisie perks up and saunters over to me, then lays down beside me.

"You really didn't like that woman, huh?" she asks.

"Doesn't matter if I liked her or not, my family matters more," I shrug. "I didn't want any of the dogs I loved to be adopted. I still don't. Not when I'm in a place that is relatively safe, and I can be around dogs I love after my home and my best friend were taken away from me in the span of a few hours."

"Right, yeah." Her voice takes on a more negative tone. Jealousy, maybe? But what would she have to be jealous about? My life had been turned upside down so fast I practically had an emotional whiplash trying to comprehend it all.

"Maisie?" I ask tentatively.

"Hm?"

"Are you… are you mad at me?"

Maisie sighs.

"In the two years you've been gone, I've been fostered by many families. Never staying in one place for more than five months, with something always happening that forced my foster family to bring me back: whether it was too much work to take care of me, or a family cat that hated my guts. I want to settle down. Be petted by kids, or an older woman, or a college student who's really busy but loves me and takes time out of their day to make sure I know I'm loved. And you took that possibility from me."

Before I can interrupt, Maisie ploughs on.

"I know you love me. I've known it from the pain in your eyes when we split the last time, and in the excitement you felt when you saw me again after two years. But if I'm adopted, or if you are, we might never see each other again. For real, this time. And I'll miss you, of course, but I can't stay here with you just because you want me to. If I get the opportunity to be adopted… well, I'll take it. I'm tired of transitions. Tired of the endless back-and-forths. Just thought you should know."

My heart feels like it's being dissolved in stomach acid. I never thought about that. And I feel like the worst friend in the world for doing that to Maisie. A lump builds up in my throat.

"Maisie, I'm… I'm so sorry…" Maisie nods.

"Don't worry about it too much. She won't be the last person coming in to adopt a dog, and that means you still have me here for a little while. Come on, don't cry. Such is life, y'know?"

Such is life indeed. But if life is as such, why does it have to be so hard?

I swallow and force a cough to get the lump out of my throat. I plaster a fake (but hopefully believable) smile on my face.

"Yeah. Such is life."

CHAPTER 5: ONE BY ONE

It started with Wally.

A week after mine and Maisie's conversation, a tall, thin, balding man walked in, with Mike opening the door for him. The man saw Wally, pointed at him, and said 'that one' without a moment's hesitation. Wally grinned and walked over to the man, winding around his ankles. The balding man laughed and picked him up, and it was clear he was thoroughly enjoying it.

"Wally, are you sure you want to live with him? You barely know the man!" Darrell asked, his voice strained. I know Darrell had known Wally well. Their relationship was a little bit like mine and Trey's, at least from what I knew.

"He seems fine. He looks friendly enough—ooh! Treat!" Mike was holding out a hand with a treat, and Wally snatched it up, smacking his lips together once it had been eaten. "Is there more?" He began sniffing around, his long nose bobbing up and down in his efforts. Darrell let out a broken laugh at that.

"Are you *really* sure you trust him, though? Remember how you told me your last owner was bald? Maybe this guy will be as bad as he was!" I could hear the desperation in Darrell's voice, and I had to remind myself to be strong in this moment. Not to ruin it for Wally like I did for Maisie.

"Darrell, buddy, don't be ridiculous. Bald people aren't all bad, just like how all people with hair aren't always good. He's pretty gentle and he has a nice smile. He smells like… that flower that you showed me where I almost inhaled a bee trying to smell it… the blue one…"

"I remember."

"Maybe he's a gardener! That sounds so relaxing, and I could really do with some relaxing right about now."

"True. You deserve to get the relaxing you want, all the relaxing in the world, but… I would give up all the turkey legs in the world if it meant that I'd get to be with my best friend for just a little while longer."

"Darrell, buddy, I never knew you could be so eloquent! Don't worry. Maybe we'll see each other again. Maybe we'll even live next door to each other, wouldn't that just be great? Keep your hopes up. There's still time."

Darrell nodded.

"I'll keep hoping 'till I die, Wally, old pal. Enjoy your relaxing."

"You bet I will! Bye, y'all!" I raised a paw in goodbye, and soon the rest of the dogs followed my example. Darrell's paw was the last to go up. As Wally was being carried out in his new owner's arms, I heard a 'bye, Wally, I love you' escape Darrell's mouth. And once the door closed, he made a noise like he'd been punched in the gut. I couldn't bear to watch him.

How many more adoptions would I have to sit through? How many more dogs would I have to lose? And how many more dogs would have to sit there too, powerless, as they watched those they loved leave?

Too many. Way too many.

Wally leaving was a blow to everyone from the Den, but Darrell was taking it hardest of all. He ate fine, he slept normally (more or less), and was still Happy Uncle Darrell to the pups. Despite that, we could all see that he was getting a little more reserved, not participating as much in conversation, hanging out in the background. I hated seeing him this way.

It got me wondering what everyone thought about my reaction to Trey's death. Thinking about her left a hole in my heart that I fear may never be filled. I had dreams almost every night where I would wake up with her last scream in my head, and after discussing it with M, Brescia, and Scar, it turns out I wasn't alone in that. I had gotten much more reserved, and more easily aggravated, than ever before. I wondered if Scar and Brescia—and the other dogs from the Den, for that matter—felt the same way about me as I am now feeling about Darrell. But they were still there to support me.

I decided to walk over to Darrell and see how he was doing.

"Oh, hey, Comet," he said upon noticing me walk over. His eyes were open wide, but were without the twinkle that had been there ever since I'd met him. "How are you doing?"

"Don't worry about me, Darrell, how are *you*?" I asked. Darrell heaved a sigh.

"Oh, I'm doing alright. Wally was my friend, you know, but after all, we're dogs in a world built for and by humans. I was stupid to get so attached."

"You were *not* stupid. Trey is gone from us. But when we were with her, we were happy... at least most of the time. I don't regret the time I spent with her, and you shouldn't regret being Wally's friend just because he's gone now."

"Well, gee, guess you're right, Comet. Smart cookie, you are," Darrell said, and I felt a wave of happiness wash over me as a small sparkle came back to Darrell's eyes. "I'm old, Comet. I don't think I have much time left, maybe a couple of years at most. It'd be nice if I could get adopted before I go. It'd spare the rest of you seeing me pass, 'specially the lil ones. You've lost enough folks already."

The small sense of joy I had was wiped away almost as fast as it came.

"Darrell, don't talk like that. You still have time. And if you want to get adopted…" I thought about what Maisie had said about being fostered and wanting a stable home. Maybe Darrell also wanted stability, and 'relaxing' like Wally had now. "…well, I think that's a great thing for you. There's a loving human out there for you with a lovely fireplace for you to sit next to, with a big ol' dog bone."

Darrell beamed, the muscles near his eyes wrinkling up.

"Well now, that sounds great, Comet. You sure have a way with words. Boy, I wish I could describe things like you can."

I flushed and turned away, not sure how to respond. Suddenly, the door opened again, and the beefiest, most tattooed man I had ever seen opened the door.

"He sure is one… large man," Darrell whispered to me in an almost awe-like voice.

"He scares me," I replied in the same whisper. Just as I said that, the man sat down on the floor and looked at all of us. I never had the opportunity to look him properly in the eyes, but now that I did, I saw that he had the same look in his eyes that Maisie did when she saw the pups for the first time. He reached his hand out in front of him, not towards any particular dog, and waved it around, seeing who would trust him. When nobody did at first, he let his hand hang back by his side.

"Always loved dogs," grunted the man. "Had a soft spot for 'em since I was a little boy. Just so happens that I like rock music and my motorcycle too."

There was nobody else in the room, so his comment was met by silence, but the man didn't seem to mind.

"Aww, that's so sweet," murmured Darrell beside me. "I'ma go closer."

I was about to yell at him to stay, but remembered our conversation. The man's face lit up with joy at seeing Darrell walk up to him willingly.

"Would ya look at that?" he marveled. "A pit bull! Say, they're known for being violent and vicious and all that, but you… you're just a sweetheart, aren't you, ol' buddy?"

Darrell had no words. I could see he was a little overwhelmed at the man being so loving and enthusiastic over him, and just relaxed with his tongue hanging out and his tail wagging. Darrell's tail, for the first time since the fire, was *wagging*.

Scar walked over to me and leaned in close to whisper in my ear.

"What did you say to Darrell when it was just the two of you?"

"Not much," I replied. "He misses Wally. Wants a stable life while he still has time."

Scar paused to reflect for a second.

"That's right. Darrell's one of the older ones. Sometimes I forget that, since he's always been so friendly and lively."

"He gets along quite well with this guy, doesn't he?" I asked Scar.

"Yeah, he definitely does."

"Alright, as much as I'd love to be petting you, I gotta go sign some papers. I'll be back, buddy, okay? You're coming home with me, how does that sound?" The tattooed man stood up and grinned like a kid in a candy store. Darrell barked excitedly. No words, just bark. I thought I was going to be upset, but I found myself grinning, and when I looked at Scar, I saw that he was too.

Darrell came prancing over to us. I bet he felt like he was in the clouds, weightless with joy.

"How did it go?" I asked once Darrell stopped in front of us. His tongue was hanging out of his mouth and the sparkle in his eyes was so bright they could've been stars of their own. "You seemed to get along quite well."

"Oh, he was so nice! He gives the greatest pets, and oh! I bet he gives great hugs too!" Darrell looked back towards the doorway where the man came from, tail wagging and eyes open wide.

"You're lucky, Darrell," said Scar softly. "We're so happy for you."

Darrell and I looked towards Scar to see him with a bowed head and a sad smile. He looked up at us both and let out a laugh that was so ridiculously faked. I suppose it's better to laugh than cry.

"I'll definitely miss all of you guys," said Darrell. "Chin up, Scar. There, that's better. The Den's been an amazing experience, and all of you are my true family, forever and always. But as I've told Comet, I'm getting old. I'd like to spend my last years not having to be so focused on survival, and getting some peace and quiet."

"And you should *absolutely* get that. We're so grateful to have had you as a part of our lives, Darrell." This was Brescia, who heard part of our conversation and joined in.

I decided not to say as much. I just wanted to be there for Darrell, and for my parents, as they said their final goodbyes.

"Darrell, before you go, would you like to say goodbye to the pups?" Scar asked softly. Darrell froze.

"Oh, gee, it's going to break the little one's hearts to see Ol' Uncle Darrell go. But it's better they get a true good-bye and not me slipping away behind their lovely little backs."

Scar called the pups over and they raced over excitedly. My heart sank as I knew that their excitement would fade.

"Uncle Darrell's got something to tell you guys," Brescia murmured into their furs. She then looked up at Darrell and nodded once, firmly, but not harshly.

"Well, I've sure been put in the spotlight," chuckled Darrell as the pups sat on their hind legs and watched him expectantly. "But, here we go. Little ones, Uncle Darrell's going to be adopted now." The pups' mouths fell open in shock.

"You're *leaving*?" asked Ellie incredulously.

"Will we ever see you again?" asked Tina.

"We'll miss you!" said Dusty, his lower lip trembling.

"Yes, Uncle Darrell's leaving. But maybe he'll see you again!" I knew Darrell was only saying this so that the pups wouldn't be too heartbroken, but it was an empty promise. He could die before they'd have the opportunity to see him, or they could be living in completely different neighbourhoods for the rest of their lives.

"I know it's sad, but that's what happens sometimes. We get adopted and there's nothing anyone can do to stop it," explained Brescia calmly. Dusty let out a small whimper — just one.

"Can we have one last hug goodbye?" he asked.

"Of course!" said Darrell joyfully. "Bring it in." The pups immediately hugged Darrell's legs and held on tight. Scar, Brescia and I watched, hanging a little bit in the background.

"You guys too, come on now, don't leave me hanging," said Darrell with a cheeky smile. We all gathered in and hugged for a good long while. Finally, the hug broke as

Darrell's new owner came in and scooped him up in one large hand.

"Bye everybody! I'll miss you!" The door closed, and that was the last I saw of Darrell for a long, long time.

Darrell's adoption had been one of my hardest goodbyes. But coming in close second was the day that both M and Maisie were adopted. It was on the same day, and at the same time, but by two completely different families.

M was spotted first. She was a pretty young dog, what with her show dog background and all, and well-behaved too. So it was no surprise that when a family with a baby and a shy three-year-old showed up, they immediately took a liking to her.

Maisie, on the other hand, was spotted by a young woman in her twenties who was wearing the shortest dress I had ever seen. She walked in, and it wasn't an immediate "love-at-first-sight" reaction, but after the woman got to know us, she started getting more attached to Maisie.

M's future owner left the room with the kids, who at this point were starting to get bored and were about to throw a tantrum. Maisie's owner was sitting on the floor, petting her slowly and steadily. Maisie was ecstatic.

"I can't believe it. I was so mad at you for keeping me from that first woman, but now I realise that maybe it was fate or something! I love this new woman, she's so kind and sweet, and she gives great pets!" she exclaimed. My heart dug itself a hole somewhere between my ribs and lodged there. There was a pretty big chance I would never see Maisie ever again, which was really upsetting to think about, but I didn't want to keep her from what she truly wanted. What kind of friend would I be if I did that?

"Well... you're welcome, I guess?" I replied jokingly. "I hope you'll be happy. Promise me you'll take care of yourself? Make new friends, relax and enjoy a life filled with the kind of unconditional love you deserve."

"I never thought I'd be living with kids," M brought up. "I've never lived with kids before, and I *definitely* didn't think I'd be living with kids this young. But as long as they're good to me, I'll be happy living with them."

"Oh yeah, I never thought about kids, ever. Maybe my new owner will have kids in the future! Living with a baby though... that sounds *weird.* Something I'll definitely have to get used to," Maisie added.

"I don't think it'll be that different from getting used to the pups," I said. "They slept a lot, and whined, and needed a lot of attention: especially Dusty, what with the being-born-dead-at-first kinda thing. And they couldn't really communicate very well, at least for the first few months."

"I guess that's fair. But I won't ever be able to communicate with a human baby, even when it grows," replied Maisie.

"True."

At that point, M's owner came into the room again. One kid had really red eyes and his lower lip was trembling, which made me think he'd probably just had a tantrum outside. But it also seemed like the tantrum was over because the mom let him down to the floor, and he waddled over to M, looking nervous but also with his hand out like he wanted to pet my friend.

M, noticing this, grinned at me and walked over to the kid, winding around him and making sure her fuzzy tail wound around him too. The kid began giggling and laughing, petting M and waving his arms around happily. I remembered M telling me and Brescia about her past all those years ago, and I looked over to see that her fur had grown to the point that the scar across her back was covered. Whether anyone could see it or not, that scar would always be a part of her: a memory of what she had lived through. A sign of her resilience. I wondered if the humans saw it at all. I wondered if they cared.

Maisie's new owner stood up and walked over to the kid's mom.

"The shelter workers are ready for you now," said the kid's mom. "Congrats on your new dog!"

"Thanks! You too!" replied Maisie's new owner.

Maisie's owner left, and it was just me and her now.

"We've had a great many experiences together, and I'll never forget you," I began, my voice choking up. There were so many things I found myself wanting to say, but my voice didn't seem to work, and my brain wasn't putting enough words together to properly express what I wanted to say.

"Comet, I'll never forget you either, and that's a fact. No matter how old I get, I will remember all the highs and lows we've had. And who knows, there's always a chance I'll see you again, either walking with another owner or at the dog park, or who knows!"

"Maisie, how do you stay so hopeful?"

"One of us has to be. I don't want your last memories of me to be upsetting. Same with M, since after today, all your old friends will have been adopted or…"

"Or dead, Maisie, say it how it is." The thought of Trey gave me another lump in my throat, but this was not the time. "You're right. Let's make this a happy goodbye. A 'see-you-later', if you will."

"What should we do?"

"Well… what did we do when we were younger?"

"We did a lot of talking… we went on walks…"

"Alright, then. M, c'mere!" Maisie yelled. M's ears pricked up and she approached us.

"What is it?" she asked.

"We're going to have our potential last moments together be happy ones. Let's get in a huddle, and just talk like we're pups again and don't have any real future plans," explained Maisie.

"Alright, sure, I'm down."

So we laid there, and we talked, and we laughed, and we cried. And we caught up on things we'd missed, and we reminisced on memories we'd lived through together. Brescia and Scar caught on to what we were doing and joined in. M talked about how Brescia and I saved her life all those years ago. Maisie and I embarrassed Brescia – again – talking about when she had to have a bath in the shelter. Scar told us another Snuffie story.

But in the end, I remembered that it was a goodbye conversation, whether I wanted it to be or not. When M's and Maisie's owners came in with dog carriers to take them home, we did a three-way forehead touch, exchanging breath with our eyes closed, savouring the moment.

"I love you both so, *so* much. I'll miss you more than anything, but I know you'll have an amazing life with a loving family. I feel like I'm going to get choked up again, but I don't want you to see me cry, not now, not when we've made so much effort to make this a potential see-you-later instead of a full goodbye."

Maisie laughed and swished her tail pointedly a few times.

"I will. And I'll miss you, as I've said. And you'll always be my best friend."

"Mine too," replied M. "Always and always. I love you."

Brescia and Scar said their goodbyes separately. They had a different perspective and relationship with the two of them than I did, and I was fine letting them be for the time being. I also didn't want to add too many words in my goodbye. I wanted it to be simple, and I wanted them to know that no matter where we were in life, I would remember them and hold a special place for them in my heart. And I think I managed to do just that quite well.

Maisie and M left in the carriers, yelling goodbyes to everyone. I couldn't help it, and yelled one last "Goodbye! I'll miss you! I love you!" Then the doors shut, and they were gone.

CHAPTER 6: SCARRED AGAIN

Sure is hard being lonely.

Of course, the pups are still here and so are Scar and Brescia. But it's quieter now that Darrell, M, Maisie, and everybody else are gone. The pups are eager to play… and I play with them, of course I do. What kind of sister would I be if I wasn't there for them? But there are times when I wish that we could go back to when things weren't as safe and stable, times when all my friends were still around.

Sure we were struggling, but I'd give anything to be struggling in the way we were before, not the way that we are now… with loneliness and regret and longing.

I hear Mike talking on the phone with someone as he takes us on our daily walk.

"Sure, you can adopt him." A pause. "And what about the German…" Another pause. "And the little ones? Mhm, mhm, yep. Gotcha. And…" I turn to face Mike at this point. "Understood." His voice gets heavier and more resigned.

"When would you want to come get 'em?" A longer pause.

"Right, yeah. Okay, well, talk to you later. You working tomorrow? Mhm. Bye now."

What on earth was that about?

I eat dinner alone that night, pondering over Mike's words. Of course, the "German" something is referring to Brescia. There are no German Shepherds anywhere else in the shelter, or anything German of any sort, for that matter. The little ones have to be the pups, but there are other pups in the shelter, so maybe I'm just being paranoid.

Scar and Brescia walk slowly up to me, avoiding my eyes but looking at each other sheepishly. My heart leaps in my throat as worried thoughts run through my mind. Is one of them sick? Did *I* do something? What is it?

"Hi, Comet," Brescia begins. "How… how are you?"

"I'm doing alright, I suppose. As well as I can be, considering everyone is gone," I reply, and though I try to be a little sarcastic, a little humorous, my voice comes out somewhat strained. "How are you?"

Brescia and Scar look at each other again.

"We're doing alright. Are the pups causing you any trouble?"

"No, they're not. You know I love them. They could never be a burden to me. I'd adopt them and take care of them myself if you weren't able to care for them. Not that that's something I'm hoping for but… y'know…" I reply hastily.

Scar gives a weak chuckle.

"Right, yeah." Then he turns to Brescia again. A look goes between them for the third time that I can't quite place.

"What is that look for?" I ask. "Are you going to tell me what's going on, or do I have to figure it out as some really upsetting surprise?"

Scar sighs and seems to be really avoiding looking at Brescia again. He doesn't say anything. Brescia sighs in turn and replies to my question.

"You heard Mike on the phone, yes?"

"Yeah."

"Well, what you don't know is that when we were saying goodbye to Maisie and M, and you weren't with us, we heard a little bit of Mike and Jack talking on the phone. The shelter is going through some financial troubles and with the many dogs that are still here, they're having a hard time buying all the food and necessities, alongside having to pay bills of all sorts: vet, electric, and stuff like that," Brescia begins. "Even with all the adoptions happening, it's not quite enough."

"Which means…" I prompt.

"Which means that a lot more dogs are going to be adopted in a short amount of time. Less food that the shelter needs to buy, and more money coming in for other things," Scar adds.

"I don't… what does that have to do with me?" I ask, my legs starting to shake as I fear the worst.

"Comet, love… me and your mother are getting older. Not *Darrell* older, but still, older. We haven't really had a moment's peace in a long time. Of course, we loved the Den and all its members, but even you can't deny that there've been some hard times," Scar says.

"Just tell me, so I don't make myself more nervous than I need to be!" I yell. "And stop looking at each other like that! I know it's going to be a hard thing for me to hear, but god damn it, just *tell me*! And why do you keep sighing?"

Scar snorts.

"We're trying to soften the blow but…"

"*Tell me!*"

"Comet, Jack's adopting us," Brescia cuts in.

"All of us? The…" I quickly count in my head. "With me, you two, and the pups, that's… the six of us? That's a lot of…" I trail off as Brescia shakes her head.

"Oh. Oh, no."

"This is why we wanted to soften the blow," Scar mutters under his breath. Brescia smacks him with her tail.

"Who's being adopted then? Who's *us*?" I ask frantically.

"It's just me and Brescia."

"What about the pups? They'll be devastated that their parents are leaving them in this place."

"Oh, the pups are being adopted too. Me and Scar are the ones being adopted by Jack," Brescia explains. "But the pups are going to be split with Jack's various cousins and family members. They all have kids, so the pups are going to get a lot of love. It's common with families to adopt the puppies of another family member's dog."

"*Do the pups know?*"

"Of course, we told them first. They took it easier than we thought, but that doesn't mean it isn't going to be hard for them. They'll be able to see us from time to time." Brescia's voice softens as she talks about the pups. She looks back to see them playing with each other, and she smiles.

"*Us?*" I ask. "So does that mean I'm going to live with another of Jack's family members too?"

Please say yes, please say yes. Please…

"You're staying here," Scar says bluntly.

"*WHAT? Why?*"

"Jack and Mike were discussing, and they remembered how you got violent with the woman earlier."

"Violent is an overreaction…"

"You bit her! Or tried to. They don't know you are – or were, I guess – attached to Maisie and were trying to keep her here. They don't know you've already lost Trey and don't want to lose anybody else. All they know is that you're a – likely traumatised – street dog that doesn't take kindly to humans. They're not going to house you where there are kids, especially young ones."

If I could have turned any more pale than my already grey husky fur, I would have.

"You've… you've got to be joking. The only family I have left is *leaving me*? Just like that?"

"You think we want this?" Scar asks, his raised voice beginning to crack. "Comet, I love you more than I can possibly explain. You don't know… you *can't* understand how hard this is for me as a parent. I saved your life and took you under my wing. Maybe at first it was a sense of duty, but then it became an active choice because I loved you. I *still* love you so, so much. I've seen you grow in ways I don't think you properly see in yourself. I would trust you with my life, with the pups' lives, with everything. I don't want to be separated from you. But we have no choice. We're dogs, Comet. We have to face facts, and sometimes facts hurt like hell."

I barely register half of those words because of the ringing in my ears.

"I don't… I don't even know what to say. So what's going to become of me then? Living alone in the Quiet Room for the rest of my days? Never getting adopted? Never seeing you, or anyone I know and love ever again? *What kind of life is that?*"

"I know it hurts, and I know it sucks, but that's life sometimes," says Brescia, coming closer and hugging me in whatever way she can because, as Scar put eloquently some time ago, *we're dogs*. "We love you so, so much, Comet. You're our daughter. Our firstborn… so to speak. Our pride and joy."

I get a lump in my throat.

"When do you leave? When do we have to say goodbye for good?"

"It's not goodbye for good! What was it you said to Maisie and M? That there was still hope we'd see each other again?" exclaims Brescia.

"You think I believed that? Any of it? I just said that, so I wouldn't cry and look ridiculous. I just said that to make Maisie and M happy, if happy is even the right word. I could be adopted and brought to another country for all we know! You could be dead before I get a chance to see you again!"

Scar tries to cover a sob with a cough unsuccessfully and runs from us. My heart sinks. I watch Scar's trembling body a few paces away from us.

"Comet, love…" Brescia doesn't seem to know what to say.

"Just leave me alone."

"We don't want to leave you, Comet. If we could some-how, out-of-the-blue, convince Jack's family to adopt you, we would in a heartbeat."

"Just. Leave. Me. Alone!"

"As you wish." Brescia turns to comfort Scar, and I watch her go with instant regret. What if they left tomorrow morning, before I even wake up, and this is the last thing I told them?

"No! Wait!" I break down sobbing before Brescia can look at me.

"I don't want you to leave me alone. I don't want you to go. I'm sorry, I didn't mean it."

"We know, Comet," says Scar thickly. "We know."

"I hate this! I hate it, I hate it, I *hate it*!" I yell, pressing my body against Brescia's and Scar's as if this is the last time I can ever feel their fur. Or their muscles, tight under their skin. Or their breath, the smell all too familiar. I revel in that scent and try to memorise it, keep some of that scent with me, so I can remember my parents when they're gone. Or… or…

I do my best to keep the three of us huddled together so I can keep the memory of them in my mind, and keep their comforting hugs against my skin. No matter how much they try to end the hug, I leap towards them again. Finally, Brescia speaks again.

"Comet, darling. You have to let go now."

"No."

"Comet…"

"No! Don't leave me!"

"We're not leaving just yet, love. We'll still be here until tomorrow afternoon. Jack's relatives are still getting everything ready, and we're all going to be leaving at the same time."

"I hate that the word 'we' in this situation excludes me," I say, my voice trembling, and my face buried into Scar's shoulder.

"Everyone does, Comet, but we have *no choice*."

I take a big shuddering gasp and forcibly wrench myself away from the hug. My skin feels like it's been replaced with tin foil; all cold and stiff. I am shaking as I will myself not to run back into the safety and comfort of their embrace.

The pups approach us, and I curse violently under my breath. I can't stay strong for them, and I bet this is going to make their experience getting adopted all the more difficult. They'll be leaving each other, and me, and they were so ready and so strong until now!

"Comet!" hisses Scar, and I stop cursing. The pups are looking at me curiously.

"Comet? Why are you crying?" asks Dusty. All I can think about is how I might never see his face again, the miracle pup that might not have existed if not for Brescia's love. The adoring, naive, quiet pup who melts every heart in the vicinity. It's all I can do to respond without sobbing again.

"Did Mom tell you guys? I'll be…" The remainder of this sentence plays in my head exactly how I want to say it, but something stops me. I feel like once I tell the pups, I won't be able to keep it together, and I can't burden them with having to be strong for me. I'm the eldest, I'm supposed to be the strong one.

"Comet?" Dusty repeats.

"Mom, you tell them," I plead.

Brescia sighs and nuzzles my shoulder.

"I'd say you're working yourself up, but I probably would feel the same way in your situation, so there's that. Pups, you know how we're going to be living with Jack and his many different family members?"

The pups nod at various speeds. If not for the tension in the situation, I would laugh. They look like bobbleheads.

"And remember how I told you Comet would be staying here?"

"I remember!" Ellie yelps excitedly. Then her face falls. "Oh."

She walks up to me and looks up at me with her sparkly eyes. They're not full of tears, but she definitely looks concerned.

"Are you upset that you're not coming with us?" she asks.

Forget the 'tough older sister' act.

My legs give out under me and I fall down to Ellie's height. I nod and start ugly-crying, my eyes shut tight. I bet they're all bloodshot too. They're going to hurt tonight, that's for sure.

"It's okay, we'll still love you."

I don't know whether to laugh or cry, so I end up doing both.

"Thanks… thanks, Ellie," I manage to blubber out.

"You're welcome!" And just like that, she gives me a huge lick on the side of my face, followed by the rest of the pups doing the exact same thing. Then they scamper off.

"How do you think that went?" I ask Scar and Brescia, my face probably looking absolutely hideous.

"It wasn't bad, all things considered," Scar says, trying to keep his voice chipper and enthusiastic, but I know it's fake. "Go get some rest, Comet. Maybe you'll feel better in the morning. We did drop a lot of news on you at one big moment."

"A lot of really upsetting and heartbreaking news," I mumble.

"True. But still, go to sleep, you'll feel better in the morning." The words 'I hope' hung unsaid in the air.

"Right, right." I turn to leave, but a feeling resembling panic settles in my stomach as Scar and Brescia leave my immediate line of sight.

"Can you guys be with me until I fall asleep? I don't want to lose any time with you guys, considering…" I gulp. "…considering there might not be much time left."

Brescia and Scar look at each other and nod. I lead them to the place where I've chosen to sleep, and lay down. They lay down besides me, one to my left and one to my right.

"I love you guys," I say.

"We love you too," Scar replies.

I nod and lay my head down on my paws. Brescia and Scar huddle close to me, and for a minute, I can almost forget we're on the shelter floor before a day that is sure to break me even more than I think I'm broken. I can imagine we're on the floor of the Den (before the fire, of course) and we still have tons of time together. I can imagine there's a breeze, and the sun is warming my fur. By the time I'm dreaming of this, Scar and Brescia have stood up and left me to sleep.

But it's okay. At least I'll see them in the morning, right? Right?

I panic when I wake up because I feel neither Scar's nor Brescia's warm bodies lying beside me. I jump upright as if I had been struck by lightning, and I look around frantically. Luckily, I don't have to look for too long because they're having breakfast with the pups and another dog from the shelter who I don't know very well. All I know is that her name is Willa and she's a collie.

I walk over to them. I'm drowsy, both from having just woken up and from the adrenaline fading.

"Hi Comet, how'd you sleep?" Brescia asks calmly.

"I slept alright," I mumble, trying to shake myself awake.

"That's good," she replies. "Have you met Willa?"

"In passing." I nod to her, and she gives me a small, sweet smile back. I wish I wasn't as tired or emotionally drained. We could have been good friends. I also *could* technically befriend her after Scar, Brescia, and the pups leave, but the thought of them leaving is too overwhelming to think about, consuming all other thoughts I could have.

"Willa's an ex-farm dog. After her family's farm went out of business last year, they had to let her go because they didn't have the money to take care of her anymore," Scar explains.

"Oh, that sucks," I say in an attempt to be genuine. I walk heavily over to my food and start eating it, keeping one ear available to listen to my parents.

"It does. It *did*, especially in those first few days, but then I got used to it," Willa says, chiming into the conversation.

"I bet, yeah. Sorry if I sound dead inside, for one, I am, and second of all, I'm still trying to wake up fully," I mumble between mouthfuls of food.

"That's alright, love," says Brescia with a small chuckle. "You got some kibble on your..." She walks over and starts licking me.

"Mom, stop! I got it!"

Brescia steps back, a little disappointed.

"Alright, alright." I feel my heart seize as I realise that Brescia's probably just trying to act like my mother and interact with me in any way she can before she's gone for good. Let's face it, she probably won't see me again until we're both dead. I don't reply and just continue eating. Scar walks over and stops beside Brescia.

"Love, I know you don't want to, but let's go talk to the pups, get them ready for their adoption time. This is their first time going through the process... god, I hope it'll be their one and only time... and I want to make sure they're really truly ready," whispers Scar just loud enough for me to hear it as well. Whether it was intentional or not, I don't know.

"You're right," replies Brescia with a sigh. "Comet, are you going to be okay here?" I nod, trying to look certain, but on the inside, I honestly don't know.

When Brescia and Scar leave, Willa sidles up to me.

"Hey, honey. How're you doing?"

I give her a sideways look.

"Everyone I know and love is either dead, gone, or leaving. I dunno, how *am* I doing?"

I probably shouldn't be rude, but I don't want to get attached to Willa. What if she gets torn from me, just like everybody else? Maybe I'll just stay quietly in my cage

73

from now on. That way, at least the only pain will be from my claustrophobia.

"I think you're feeling pretty down-in-the-dumps, aren't you? Sad, lonely, angry…" Willa trails off as I give her another sideways look, then roll my eyes dramatically.

"You don't get it."

"Try me?"

A lump gathers in my throat. I am *not* going to cry in front of this new dog. But nonetheless, something in my brain is telling me to just lay down all my troubles in front of her. Tell her everything that's been on my mind. For the hell of it. But I know in my heart that that'll end up with me getting a new friend who's more well-behaved and adoption-ready, who's going to be leaving me in another two weeks.

"No."

"Suit yourself, honey. I'll be there when you need me."

"Wait all you like. I don't need you."

Willa stands up and walks away.

Mike opens the door and everyone's eyes flick towards the entrance. He scans the room and kneels in front of Scar, Brescia, and the pups.

"Hey guys!" he chirps. "Your new owners are going to be here right after lunch, okay? There's gonna be a lot of people here, so you all gotta be on your best behaviour for the humans, okay?" I saunter over to stand beside Scar, and Mike looks at me sternly.

"If you're going to be out of the cage, Hunter, you have to promise me that you *won't bite anybody*, okay? You have one chance to be a good dog, or you'll be in the Quiet Room."

I nod and wag my tail, so Mike believes me. I don't know how much of a 'good dog' I can be, but I'll do my best. My family deserves a proper send-off, no matter how much it's going to hurt me to see them go.

Our morning goes by ridiculously fast. Baths, walks, playtime, lunch, and before I know it, Jack is walking through the front door with a bunch of people who look kinda like him, who I assume are his various relatives. I stand there in shock as they bend down to pet the pups.

I want to run over and defend the pups, but these people are harmless. They're going to give the pups a good home, and I promised Mike and myself that I'd be a 'good dog'. So even though my claws are out, and my jaw is clenched, I don't move. I just watch in horror as everything unfolds.

Jack kneels down and pets Scar and Brescia behind the ears. For a minute, they look years younger as they smile and accept the pats. Something pulls at my heartstrings, and I don't know what it is. Is it that they're going to be gone, and I'm preparing myself for that heartbreak? No, it's something else. What is it?

Willa comes up to me, and I don't notice her until she speaks, causing me to jump in surprise.

"You jealous that you can't be petted like that?"

"What?! No! That's impossible! No, absolutely not. Nuh-uh. Nope."

"Right." She lets the 'i' draw out for way longer than it needs to.

I roll my eyes, causing her to smile sadly and walk away from me again.

"Max, buddy, you and your family are going to be so safe and so loved with us," Jack says. "We'll take such good care of you guys."

Suddenly, an idea hits me. Maybe if I can prove to the humans that I'm lovable enough and ready to be adopted, Jack's family can still take me, and I don't have to be separated from everyone! It might not work, but it's my last chance.

I walk up to Jack and look up at him with big puppy-dog eyes.

"Hey, Hunter, how are you doing?" Jack says excitedly. Resentment starts to simmer in my stomach, but I can't let that show. I need these people to like me.

Jack reaches his hand out to pet me, and for once, I let him.

Scar, behind me, lets out a chuckle.

"Good to see you happy again, Comet."

I smile, not responding. Soon, Jack's pets stop and he stands up.

"I'm going to talk to my family now, guys, I'll be back."

I stand silently next to Scar and Brescia as we watch Jack's nieces and nephews (or whatever relatives those are) play with the pups excitedly. They seem a little nervous, but they're gentle, and so are the pups. I've realised that I'm not nervous about the homes that the pups will go to. They'll be very well cared for. I'm more concerned about how *I'm* going to be once they're gone. But that's a thought for another time.

Jack and the other adults of his family are talking to each other. I catch a little bit of what they're saying.

"…the husky…"

"…Mike says she bites…"

"…seems okay…"

"…sign papers now…"

That's about all I hear before they step out of the room. Scar and Brescia haven't noticed, they're just watching the human kids play with the pups, like the proud parents they are.

"Mom. Dad. Mom. Dad. Scar. Brescia. Guys," I say, trying to get their attention.

"Mm?" Brescia asks.

"They were talking about me. The humans. The adults. Maybe they'll adopt me."

"Maybe. But… and I know this is going to sound terrible… Adopting a dog is a big decision for a family, especially with kids. If you've bitten someone, the trust goes way down, and it takes a lot more time than already has gone by to get that trust back," explains Scar.

I sigh, another lump growing in my throat.

"God, I wish I hadn't bitten that woman, or tried to anyway! I was so stupid, I've ruined everything! I've…"

"Comet, love, gimme a hug." I bury my face in Brescia's shoulder and sob.

"I know, I know, and there's no way we could have predicted that things would happen so fast, and in this manner. We still love you, no matter what," Brescia adds.

"Alright," I sob. "I love you guys too. I'm going to say goodbye to the pups."

I walk over to the pups, and the kids immediately stand up and move away from us. Their parents must have warned them about me. Is my reputation now tarnished as the dog who tried to bite someone? I'm ashamed of myself, but I put on a happy face for the pups.

"Hey guys," I say in what I think is a happy voice. "Are you liking your new owners so far?"

"I do! I do!" Ellie squeaks. "She pets us really nice, and her hair is soft when it hits me in the face by accident!"

"I think I'm going to like my owner too," says Tina. "She's kinda quiet, but she's really gentle."

"My owner is nice, too," says Dusty. "He's easily excitable, but I think it's gonna be nice living with him."

I can feel my eyes prickling like I'm about to cry, but I take a deep breath and force myself to keep talking.

"Well, you guys seem really excited about your new homes! And guess what, you'll be able to see each other sometimes! Isn't that great?" All the pups start nodding enthusiastically.

"We're gonna miss you, Comet," says Dusty. I bow my head down, my lip trembling.

"I'm going to miss you so much, too, my little miracle brother. And my lovely sisters too. You're going to have the most amazing lives with your new families."

"And if not, you can EAT THEM!" Ellie squeals. I laugh despite myself.

"Yes, Ellie, if anything happens, I will happily eat your owners. Head to toe."

Just then, the adults come back into the room with dog carriers. I lick all of my siblings with a goodbye kiss before Ellie is scooped up first, and yips at us happily as she soars off into the unknown.

"Bye Mom and Comet and Dad and Dusty and Tina and Willa and…" We all say our goodbyes, and finally, she is behind the door and out of sight.

Next is Tina.

"Bye, everyone! I'll miss you!" The door shuts, and she is gone.

Finally, Dusty gets in the third dog carrier. I look at him through the mesh. I don't envy him being in the small bag, but I do wish I were going to a loving home, which I might never get. I am now the 'Dog Who Almost Bit Someone' apparently. Maybe even the 'Dog Who Bit Someone', depending on how they decide to spin the tale. I've ruined my chances. Might as well get used to it.

"Miracle brother. Dusty-boy. I love you, and I'll miss you so much," I whisper.

"Bye, Comet."

The last time I will ever hear my only brother's soft voice say my name. I force a smile as Scar and Brescia say their goodbyes before Dusty is whisked up, up and away.

Scar and Brescia will not be in dog carriers, but on leashes. They'll be going in the back of Jack's car.

"I wish I had more time to spend with you, I wish I'd snuggled with you more, I wish I'd gone hunting with you more, I wish… I wish…" I stammer. "I wish I'd told you 'I love you' more, I wish I'd given you more kisses, I wish…"

"You've been the most beautiful daughter we could ever wish for, Comet. No more 'I wish'-es. Our time together was amazing. Don't ever downplay that," says Brescia. "Head high. Be strong. We love you."

Scar doesn't say anything big or dramatic or inspiring. He comes close to me, licks my forehead, then sighs as he looks at me.

"It seems like just yesterday I found you in that box. Now look at you. Don't lose your spark, Comet," he says softly.

"I'll do my best," I say with a shrug.

Jack bends down and clips leashes on to Scar's and Brescia's collars.

"Alright, are you guys ready to go to your new home?" he asks.

"Ready as we'll ever be, right, love?" Brescia says in her beautiful, rich voice. I might never hear it again.

"Of course." Scar and Brescia follow Jack out the door.

"Bye Mom! Bye Dad! I love you!" I call out.

"Love you too! Bye!"

The door shuts behind them. Maybe it's just me, but it seems like it shut harder than for the pups?

For a few seconds, I just stand there. Saying nothing, thinking nothing. Then it hits.

"They're gone. They're gone, they're really gone, they're…" I rush towards the door, scratching at it and sobbing.

"MOM! DAD! PUPS! MAMA! DAD! COME BACK! I NEED YOU! COME BACK!" I sob, I scream, I scrape at the door. Willa runs up to me, concerned.

"Comet, love, come away from the door, come here, it's okay, you'll be okay…"

"MOM! DAD! SCAR! BRESCIA! COME BACK!"

"Comet, come away from the door."

"I WANT MY MOM AND DAD BACK!"

"I know, sweetheart. I know."

I turn and sob into Willa's shoulder.

"My mom and dad are gone, Willa, they're gone, they're really, truly gone, and... and I'll never... I'll..." I hiccup and cry, and I bet I look gross and disgusting, but I don't care. All I know is that my parents are gone, and no matter how much I want them back, they're gone.

"It's alright, dearie, cry it out. There's nothing wrong with missing your folks."

"I want... I want my mom and dad..." I sob. At this point, I'm basically incoherent. Willa stands there and lets me cry into her shoulder. Finally, I pass out from exhaustion, and the last thing I see is Willa letting me down to the floor softly, and laying down beside me.

The last thing I think is that I don't want any new friends. I don't want a new family, either. I wish today didn't happen. I wish Trey were alive. I wish the Den were still around. I wish everything bad that happened in the past months leading up to today had never happened.

I want my mom and dad back.

PART 2: SCAR

Chapter 7: Past, Present, Future

I can hear Comet's sobbing behind the door. It's faint, but it's definitely there. I turn to Brescia, who looks very uncomfortable with her leash but is bearing it.

"You hear it, don't you?" I ask.

"Of course I hear it. There's nothing we can do about it now," she replies. The sobbing dies down and all there is now is soft whimpering to be heard amidst the busy silence of the shelter.

"Maybe we shouldn't have told her…"

"Scar, don't be delusional," Brescia says, rolling her eyes. "It would only have made it worse. If we didn't tell her earlier, she wouldn't have been able to give the pups their good send-off, and goodness knows it would have just made things much harder in the end."

"You're right, as usual. I'm just worried for Comet. She'll be having a hard time no matter what, but I hope she'll be okay. If not now, then at some point."

Brescia doesn't say anything. She just nods.

"I must be the only dog in the universe who hates collars and leashes and stuff. Do you ever end up getting used to it? It feels so… unnatural!" she blurts out after a little pause.

I chuckle and walk over to her as much as I can, given my own leash is tied to a chair that's bolted to the ground. There's a little pressure on my neck, but it doesn't hurt.

"You must not remember the feeling, but you had an owner in the past. You'll get used to it in no time," I explain. Brescia snaps at her leash for a little bit before inevitably giving up.

"Right, yeah. Can't believe I forgot."

"I don't remember my last adoption taking this long," I comment.

"Last time it was just you and Jack. Now there's me and the pups to consider. That's probably what's going on," Brescia replies.

"These conversations are pointless," I say, laying down with a *flop* on the floor. "I'm just trying to fill the silence, and it's not doing any of us any good. I just… I don't even know. I want Comet here, but if we see her right now, it's gonna just make the next goodbye worse."

"Jack will be here soon," Brescia replies. "At least I hope so." She stands tall, her ears flicking back and forth. Her eyes dart everywhere, scanning the room. I wonder how long it'll take her to break that vigilance. She's needed it for so long.

Jack comes in the door and sees me and Brescia waiting.

"Hey guys! Pups are all ready, now it's just the three of us. Max, bud, remember when I let you go the last time?" I nod slowly. "Well, I told you that you'd be welcome back whenever you need it. Not gonna lie, I'm glad you're back with me, but it's unfortunate what had to happen to your old home. I'll make sure you're comfortable in any way you need. You and your…" Jack looks to Brescia, unsure of what our relationship is.

"Watch him think I'm your mother," Brescia mutters through her clenched jaw. It takes all my energy not to laugh.

"…your friend," Jack finishes uncertainly. Brescia rolls her eyes.

"Close enough."

Jack unties our leashes and I can't fight the urge to look back at the door that would take me to Comet. Brescia gets between me and the door and turns my head away from it.

"Come on. We have to go."

"Yeah. Let's go."

Jack leads us outside and opens the car door for us. I let Brescia jump up into the back seat first, then I follow suit. The slamming of the door behind me makes her flinch.

"I can't believe I'm saying this, but I'm out of my element," Brescia says nervously. "I haven't been around humans this much in… well, in a long time."

"Don't worry, we're in this together. We can get through anything. We survived so much, what's a human house going to do to us?"

"I'm so glad we're together," Brescia says gently. "It's times like these when I remember why I married you." I feel my face go hot and look down at my paws as the car starts driving.

"Right, yeah. Thanks," I answer awkwardly, getting a laugh out of Brescia, the first genuine one since we had to announce to Comet that… well. I push thoughts of Comet out of my head. I make a promise to myself that I'll give myself time for missing her, but later. Not now, in Jack's car.

The car lurches to a stop in front of a new house some time later.

"This… this isn't…" I trail off, looking through the front window of the car (Is that what a windshield is?). The house is bigger than I remember, a completely different shape and colour, and it has a front yard too. "I'm confused, why are we here?"

"Welcome home!"

Home?

"You probably don't remember this place – why would you – but we needed more space since the family grew,"

Jack explains. "That explains the…" He waves his hand around to show the house.

"Family? *Grew*? Scar, what's going on?" Brescia asks me with a quaver in her voice.

"We're in the same boat. I'm just as confused as you are," I respond. Brescia stays very close behind me as we go inside the house.

There's no carpet in the entryway. Jack *always* had carpet in the entryway. My nails don't click on the floor since they've been clipped at the shelter, and neither do Brescia's. It's unsettling. I remember where the kitchen used to be, and I motion for Brescia to follow me. But when we get to where the arch leading to the kitchen should be, there's nothing there. My heart rate starts speeding up.

"Where are we? This isn't what I remember!" I try not to start panicking, but the new environment is stressing me out.

"Scar, calm down. He probably just moved house," Brescia says. I look at my wife and realise she's right.

"Probably. Shall we go explore, then?"

Brescia nods. I suddenly remember how much she loved exploring when we were younger. Once she became the Den Alpha, she had too much to do, and exploring a new place was not something she could do very often.

We retrace our steps to the entryway and try to locate where everything is.

As we look around, Jack sets down some food and a water bowl in the kitchen. We follow him so he can show us where he put it. I lap up a bit of water, but I'm mostly focused on my surroundings. He pats us on the back gently, and then tells us he needs to deal with something, and we should familiarise ourselves with the house. Brescia and I look at each other, shrug, and decide "why not"?

There are two bathrooms on the first floor. There was only one in Jack's old house. The main living room has a

Scattered: A Novel

fireplace, but the second one (who needs a second living room? Seems excessive) has a rug on it with a design that looks like a city, with roads and houses and cars. I didn't think Jack was the type to have a city-themed rug, but things have changed, apparently. If there are these many things on the first floor, what's it going to be like on the second? How many living rooms am I going to find in this house? Eight?

Something catches my eye as we keep wandering through the first floor of Jack's new house. It's hanging on the wall next to the bathroom door, and it's just high enough for me to see it out of my peripheral vision, but not know 100% what it is.

"Hey, Brescia, come look at this!" I call out, sitting down and staring up at the wall where the thing is hanging. Brescia slips beside me.

"What is that?" she asks. "What are we looking at?"

"Look up."

It's the photo of young me at the seaside, brought over from Jack's old place. It's a surprise that it's still here. I would've thought he'd gotten rid of it or something.

"You look so young," says Brescia. "There's something else here, did you notice?" She gets up and moves further down the hallway. I follow her, wondering what it is she's noticed. I'm not surprised there's something I've missed. She'll likely have the whole house memorised by tonight.

"What's up, what'd you notice?" I ask.

Brescia just sits down and stares at a spot on the wall, a small distance away from my seaside photo. The photo has two people kissing. One is in a suit, and one is in a dress. I can't quite see the face of the person in the dress, but I'm pretty sure they're a girl. The other is the only human I would recognize anywhere.

"Who's Jack kissing?" I ask, my eyebrows furrowing.

Brescia shrugs. "I don't know, but if they're married, which they probably are... you can tell by the white dress

87

the girl has... that means she probably lives in this house... and we'll meet her soon enough."

"How old is this picture, do you think?" I ask. Brescia shrugs again.

"Whoever this woman is, I hope she's nice," Brescia says. "After all, we'll have to live with her."

My stomach starts feeling weird, and I don't know if it's because of something I ate or what, but I don't like it. I curl up on the floor, and the more I stare up at Jack's wedding photo on the wall, and the more I wonder who this mystery woman could be, the worse I feel. Yet I can't look away, and I don't know why.

"Hey, don't worry about it," Brescia says, doing her best to console me. "You'll get used to her, just as you got used to living at the Den all those years ago."

"That's not what worries me," I say with a sigh. "I'm sure she's great, I trust Jack with my life at this point, I can trust him to marry a good, kind woman."

Brescia licks the side of my face.

"Then what does, my love?"

I sigh.

"I guess I'm just really unprepared for this. I remember Jack as living alone, in a smaller – way smaller – house, a house that *I remember from my pup-hood*, might I add... and now it feels like Jack's a completely different person."

"He's the same person he always has been," says Brescia. "Just with a little bit of... spice," she adds with a giggle. "He decided to move forward with his life, just like you and I have."

"Shall we go upstairs?" I ask, changing the topic. Brescia nods.

Upstairs, there are all the bedrooms. Jack's room is big. He's sitting at a desk here, typing away at a computer. Brescia and I jump on the bed, but Jack immediately jumps up and shoos us away. We jump off before we even have a chance to question what's going on.

"Max, no. You and Brownie aren't allowed on this bed, okay? Promise me you won't go on this bed, alright?"

"What's wrong with the bed?" Brescia whispers to me.

"I don't know," I reply. I look back at it and I notice there's a little bit of dust and dirt from our paws. I purse my lips in disapproval. "Maybe that's why, though." Brescia follows my gaze and raises her eyebrows.

"Right."

I leave the room to let Jack work, and find that there really isn't that much more upstairs. It probably would seem that there's more if there weren't so many closed doors. There are four closed doors upstairs. I'm willing to bet one is a bathroom, but I don't know what the other two would be. What other rooms would a man and his wife need?

The doorbell rings, and I freeze in my tracks, staring at Brescia, my eyes wide. She looks back at me with the same expression. We follow Jack downstairs, but stay just behind him. Maybe it's the postman – you can never trust postmen, they know where everyone lives, and that's creepy – or maybe (and this might be even worse) this might be the mysterious wife.

Mine and Brescia's heads pop out from around a corner so we can see the entryway but still be protected enough if it's someone we can't trust. Jack opens the door and his face erupts into a grin.

"Hey, baby," he says, making me want to puke all over Jack's lovely carpeted stairs. I have pet names for Brescia, sure, but I could never call her 'baby'. She'd murder me in cold blood.

A woman's voice replies. "Shh, he's asleep," she says.

Who's asleep? What in the world... Who else is here? Who else lives here?

Brescia pokes me, and I look to see the most confused and scared look on her face that I've ever seen. She mouths, *what's going on? Who's 'he'?* I shake my head, dread growing in the pit of my stomach. We both look back to Jack to see him awkwardly holding what looks a lot like just a pile of rags.

"You've got to be kidding me," Brescia mutters beside me, and I can't help but agree.

The woman steps in the house, holding a weird contraption covered in blankets and buckles that I can't even *begin* to guess what it is.

"It's Kate! Brescia, it's Kate! The girl from the shelter! From all those years ago! She's the wife! We don't have to worry anymore!" Brescia, obviously relieved, sighs and reveals herself to Kate. I follow her.

"Hi! Oh my goodness, Max and Brownie! Jack told me you were going to be here, but it's still so good to see you!" She bends down to pet us, and I can't help the excited bark that escapes my mouth. And just like that, quick as a wink, the bundle of rags starts screaming.

Chapter 8: The Child Awakens

"Scar! Look what you've done!" Brescia yelps, tearing away from the scene to get away from the infernal noise. I stay there, rooted to the spot, wondering what on earth I've done to cause this havoc.

I look wildly back and forth from Jack to Kate. They're not scared or anything, just... disappointed maybe. Tired. I'm more confused than ever... and then they start making these weird noises.

"Shhh... it's okay. Don't cry, it's okay. Shh. Hush now."
WHAT?

A smooth, skin-covered orb emerges from the bundle of rags. Jack moves the bundle around and starts gently rocking it.

Oh. Oh, no. No, no, no. This is much worse than the news about Jack's new wife. Apparently, she's not the only new person that Brescia and I are going to be living with for the rest of our lives.

There's a baby in the house.

I repeat, there is a *baby* in the house.

Jack and Kate are too busy shushing the kid to notice me. I sprint towards Brescia at full speed.

"Brescia, it's... it's..." Even the small run has me ridiculously out of breath. "It's a baby. A human baby."

Her eyes widen.

"Oh! Everything makes sense now," she breathes. "The car rug, the closed doors everywhere... the new house..."

"This is a nightmare. I was okay with the wife, but a *child*?"

"Scar, don't tell me you've forgotten that you're a parent this fast," Brescia reminds me.

"Don't be ridiculous, I haven't forgotten about our pups... or Comet." The harsh reminder of our first daughter hurts, and I let the pain rest in my heart for a little bit before continuing. "But this... this is completely different! It's not smart enough to treat us right, it's loud and smelly, and so ridiculously delicate! No sleep, no safety, no attention to us from our own owners! They couldn't wait until the kid was older?"

"A lot of kids grow up with dogs," Brescia begins. "I hear your concerns, but remember? The shelter needed the money. And... I know you and I don't want to admit it, but it must be said that we... as well as all the other dogs in the shelter... needed homes."

I huff, but I can't deny that she's right.

The child, luckily for us, has stopped crying and is giggling. Kate takes the kid in her arms and heads upstairs, closing one of the doors behind her. I wonder what she's going to do there.

Jack leaves to go upstairs again, so Brescia and I are alone again in the hallway. In silence.

"Jack and Kate are going to be great parents," I point out, trying to break the silence.

"I'm sure they already are," Brescia replies.

"How old do you think the kid is?" She shrugs.

"I don't know human ages. That thing could be anywhere from three weeks to eight months."

"Should we head outside?" I ask.

"Is there an outside we can head to?"

"I hope so."

There is an outside indeed. It's spacious – way more spacious than I thought. There's a deck above us, and a small play space made of colourful plastic and fabric. There's a small garden too, but it looks almost abandoned... nearly dried up completely. I guess it's harder to take care of plants when you're in charge of a human life.

"Where to?" Brescia asks. I shrug. There's nothing here for us. I suppose the kid is too young to play with balls, so that's out of the question. The play structure is too small and too unruly for us.

"I can't believe I'm saying this, but for once, I think it's better for us to be inside rather than outside," I say, looking around the backyard as my heart sinks.

"You're right," Brescia replies. "There's nothing for us to do out here, and if we're inside, there's at least places to explore, and people... some older, some tiny and loud."

Brescia and I look back sadly at the boring yard for one last time, then head inside.

Inside, the child is being fed. It eats a weird soupy thing that I'm willing to bet tastes disgusting, but weirdly enough, the baby is eating it all up easily. Brescia mimes gagging beside me.

"Humans really do eat the weirdest things," she says.

We soon find the TV is on in the living room. We sit on the couch (might as well take the opportunity before Jack or Kate tell us to get off) and stare at the TV blankly. There's a man in a suit talking to us beside swirling colours. He talks about things like 'fronts' and 'pressure systems' and I zone out. The colours are pretty, the voice is now just white noise in the background.

The colours disappear and the image on the screen vividly shifts to a picture of the Den burning. I gasp and look wildly towards Brescia, who seems just as shocked as I am. Her breathing is shaky, and her eyes are wide.

"Come on, let's get out of here," I begin, but Brescia shakes her head.

"No, I want to hear this. What could these people possibly have to say about the Den?" she asks. I don't know, and part of me doesn't want to hear, but I don't want to be alone. I don't want to leave Brescia alone in this big, strange house.

"The forest fire that ravaged the East side of the city outskirts last week has now been extinguished. Local authorities are allowing the public to return home safely." A picture shows up on the screen of firefighters spraying the Den with water. I can see the tree fallen across it, and a lump gathers in my throat as I remember Trey. I don't see her body, but it's clear she's dead. Nobody survives that, as much as I want to believe otherwise.

Enough, Scar. She made her choice. She sacrificed herself, knowing the dangers of the Den. She made sure that the death toll was as low as it could possibly be. Her death was not in vain.

The picture of the firefighters disappears and the Den, as well as the portion of Foggy Woods we can see, is all burnt to a crisp. It might not be empty, but it is definitely all charred to the point that if I were to tap it with my claw, I bet it'd all collapse. Brescia sucks in a breath.

"Oh wow," she breathes. "Look at the damage."

"It's crazy. But at least the fire's out, and people can go home," I add.

"We can't though," Brescia replies, and I stay silent after that.

Click.

Jack has appeared and is pointing the remote at the screen, changing the devastating image of the Den and its surroundings into what I think is a children's show. Lots of bright colours swirling everywhere, high-pitched voices, and what I think is supposed to be music, but doesn't sound like any music I know. It hurts my eyes, and apparently Brescia's too. We get off the couch and stand in the hallway.

Jack, on the other hand, sits on the couch with his kid, and neither of them seem to be affected by the show. The little one is laughing and enjoying it, while Jack looks excited to see his kid happy more than anything else. Kate comes and sits down as well, a drink in hand, and kisses Jack. Something in me boils.

Brescia's observational skills are unrivalled. She steers me away from the scene.

"Come on, Scar," she says in a low voice. "It'll do nobody any good if you attack Jack's wife."

Once the happy couple is out of sight, I sigh and flop down on the ground. Brescia flops down next to me and sighs as well. We sit in silence for a few minutes.

"You saw…" Brescia begins, her voice cracking. I don't know if she's referring to the Den, the tree, or what, but I nod.

"Of course, I saw. We were there. It feels surreal to be seeing all this again, even if we're in a safe space to do so. I feel like I should be running, hiding, counting all the Den members to see if they're all accounted for, but we can't because that's all in the past now," I say. I can feel my heart racing and I have to take deep breaths to calm it down. I can feel Brescia's heart racing too.

"It was our home. For so long. And we couldn't save it," Brescia says. "I miss Trey. I thought it'd be easier this time, but everything – all the memories – are coming back to me, and…" Her voice cracks again, and this time she can't get control of it again. "I wish she…"

"Me too. God, Brescia, me too." She stands there, shaking with tears that she is refusing to let out. I come close to her so she can lay her head on my shoulder, and that's when the dam breaks.

Brescia's crying stops, and she collects herself just in time for Jack to notice us in the hallway.

"We're going to watch a movie now, do you guys wanna come?" he asks. Brescia and I stare at each other, then decide, 'sure, why not?'. It'll make it easier to take our minds off of what we've seen today.

We follow Jack back into the living room and sit on the floor in front of the couch since the couch is all taken. Jack clicks the remote a couple of times and sure enough, the movie turns on. Kate goes across the room to dim the lights, narrowly missing stepping on my tail as she walks back. I look at her, and I'm tempted to give her a warning growl, but she pets my head and my tail starts wagging as if I have no control over it.

We haven't gotten ten minutes into the movie when the kid starts crawling over the couch. Back and forth, back and forth so many times it's crazy.

"Ow!" Brescia yelps, and I turn my head around towards her so fast, it's a miracle I don't have whiplash. She moves a little further from the couch so she can scratch her head.

"What happened?" I ask.

"The… stupid…" Brescia rubs her head one last time, then shakes herself out. "The stupid kid kicked me in the head. Don't… Scar, I'm *fine*. Don't attack the kid."

"I wasn't going to, who do you think I am?"

"Just making sure." She then moves back to sit next to me, but her head is leaned a little more forward, towards the screen. "I missed something, why are they dancing now?"

Sure enough, the characters on screen are dancing, whirling around to some nice music. I shrug.

"Guess I missed it too," I answer. "Maybe if we watch for long enough, we'll find out."

Five minutes later, the kid is crying.

"My ears hurt," I complain. I lay down all the way on my stomach and attempt to cover my ears with my paws.

"I wish it was a puppy, so then at least its crying wouldn't be so ugly to listen to."

"Let's get out of here, I don't think we're going to be able to watch this movie anymore," Brescia suggests. I get up from my lying position only to get *bonked* aggressively on my head by a small fist. I yelp in pain and run out of the room.

"How does that thing carry so much violence in it in such a small body?" I wonder aloud. Brescia shrugs.

"I need air," she announces. "Come on."

I follow her outside. She takes a big breath of air, her eyes closed, and her general expression shows that she is at peace.

"I love the smell of nature," she says.

"Nature? What nature?" I ask. "We are in the middle of the city."

Brescia opens her eyes at that and frowns at me.

"That's one way to ruin a moment." I'm about to apologise when she smiles. "I'm kidding. I'm just… there's enough nature to smell it and yet not enough at the same time. There's car exhaust among the maples and cigarette smoke among Kate's dying tulips, but at least here there *are* dying tulips, you know?"

"Yeah, I suppose you're right," I say. I close my eyes and breathe in the mixed city-nature smell. I'll admit it's a little fresher than simply city smell.

A short while later, Jack comes out into the backyard to call us inside. The sun at this point is starting to set, and the summer evening chill is starting to roll in as well. We follow Jack inside, and he leads us to two new doggy beds in the second living room.

"Here's where you guys will be staying," he says. "I hope it's comfortable enough."

Brescia crawls into her green doggy bed, walks in a small circle a couple of times to get comfortable, and lays down. Her tail hangs off the side and onto the cold hardwood floor. My bed is right next to hers, about the same size but my favourite colour: grey. I'm so glad Jack remembered.

"I can't believe it was only yesterday that we were at the shelter," says Brescia softly.

"It was yesterday?" I blurt out.

Brescia shakes her head.

"I love how oblivious you are," she says with a chuckle. My face grows warm, and it takes me a few minutes to be able to talk normally again.

"How do you think Comet's doing back there?" I ask. Brescia lifts her head up off her paws and sits up straight.

"Well, I hope she's doing alright," she says dubiously. "I mean, she was pretty rough when we left, but maybe things will get better for her now that she's had some time?"

"Sweet dreams, Comet, wherever you are," I whisper. Brescia mumbles something I can't catch, then lays down and goes back to sleep. I watch her steady breathing and the rise and fall of her chest for a bit before I, too, lay my head down to sleep.

I sleep well… but not for long.

A heartbroken wail sounds throughout the house, echoing and bouncing off every wall. Brescia sits bolt upright, looking quickly back and forth to see where the sound is coming from. I open my eyes slowly and try to bury my head in my doggy bed, to no avail. All that ends up happening is the wail getting distorted through the fabric.

"What kind of alarm or siren is going off?" I ask.

"I don't think it's anything like that," Brescia says in an annoyed voice, settling back down. The wail is now just a background noise among our conversation. "I think it's the baby."

"We can try to go back to sleep," I suggest. "The baby's not yours, you don't have to do anything about it."

"You're right," Brescia says with a *harrumph*. "I guess I'm just so used to the pups and their demands at night that it's ingrained in me somehow that I have to do my duty as a mother."

"I don't think it's just the pups. You were also taking care of the entire Den as an Alpha. Whenever anyone needed anything, you were there. You need your *rest*," I explain gently.

"Rest. Right." Brescia slumps down on the doggy bed. The wail is quieter now, but maybe that's just because we're used to it.

As we try to fall asleep again, we are rudely awoken by the kitchen light streaming into our living room right next door, so to speak. Brescia lets out an 'agh' as she is temporarily blinded. I bury my face in the doggy bed again and see sparkly kaleidoscope colours everywhere before I lift my head.

A bleary-eyed Kate is walking into the kitchen, bouncing a crying baby and making shushing, calming noises.

"Shh… Rowan, it's okay, shh… Rowan, my boy, come on, don't cry," Kate continues on. Slowly, the kid is calming down and the wails subside.

I hear gurgling noises and happy giggles, and Kate seems relieved. Brescia and I look at each other, also relieved. Her eyes are closing.

"Sleep, Brescia, my love. It'll do nobody any good if you keep yourself awake."

Brescia gives a soft chuckle before yawning.

"It'll do me no good if the baby keeps waking me up every few hours, but I'll do my best."

She curls up and falls asleep.

If there's any god that will hear the prayers of a dog, I pray that Brescia can sleep well tonight. Goodness knows, she deserves some peace.

Soon after, I fall asleep, and my last thoughts are that if the kid wakes us up again I will... I will... I'm too tired to think of a proper consequence.

CHAPTER 9: DOGGY PLAY DATE

Luckily, Brescia and I get to sleep for the whole night from there. We wake up to the sun shining brightly on our fur and warming us up comfortably. Brescia jumps awake, at first defensive and unsure of where she is.

"Hey, Brescia, it's okay," I tell her. "We're safe here. We're at Jack's, remember?"

"Jack's… oh, yes. The baby, and the big new house," she replies, calming down. "I wonder if there's food."

"There should be. Let's go find out."

We walk into the kitchen to see our two dog bowls filled with kibble. None of them are labelled, and they're both silver.

"I guess we just pick whichever one we want?" I wonder aloud.

"I suppose so."

The next week goes on pretty smoothly. We go on scheduled walks. The baby, Rowan, cries and doesn't really do much else, but we're learning to deal with him. He can be cute sometimes, and reminds us of our pups… and Comet. I wonder how they're all doing.

One warm weekend, Jack clips on our leashes and tells us we're going somewhere fun. We haven't really been anywhere besides our neighbourhood walk around a couple of blocks, and it's exciting to see where else we can go.

Brescia, Jack and I pile into the family car and soon we're off. I like to watch the houses fly by, and sometimes catch glimpses of what's going on inside them through the big living room windows. At one point, I saw a couple dancing in their living room without a care in the world. I'm glad they're happy. I wonder when it'll be that Brescia and I will be able to have that same carefree energy. If that's even possible after so long.

Brescia likes to look out of the front window (windshield?) of the car, as if she were the one driving. If we were human, I think she'd make the better driver, but I digress. I think part of it is the comfort that comes from knowing where we're going, and it sucks that after so long of being in charge and in control, she still thinks she has to know everything about every outing, every plan. Maybe after we live long enough at Jack's, she can learn to live and be more relaxed.

Jack keeps driving, and soon the car slows down and stops at the side of the street.

"It's hard to find parking here in the city, so we're gonna have to walk for a bit before we get there," Jack says. "But that's okay, you guys like walks, right?"

Jack grabs our leashes, locks the car, and we follow him down the sidewalk. People have to move aside for us because when there's a grown man walking with two pretty decent-sized dogs, you take up a lot of space. And when there's Brescia eyeing everyone we pass with distrust, people will steer clear from that too.

Soon I start to recognize where in the city we are. Brescia seems to recognize it too.

"Hey, isn't the shelter not far from here?" I ask.

"Yeah, I think we passed the road that leads there a few minutes ago," Brescia replies.

"And I think the Den is a few minutes away in that direction," I add, nodding my head towards it. Brescia just nods.

We turn away from the direction of the Den and go a little deeper into the city. The buildings start thinning out, and there are mostly stores and small restaurants in this part of town. And right smack-dab in the centre of it all is the dog park.

Brescia stares at me in amazement, and her tail starts wagging. I don't think I remember the last time I've seen her tail wag.

"Dog park!" she exclaims. "We're going to the dog park!"

I can't help grinning at her almost child-like excitement. I wonder how long it's been that Brescia can genuinely have fun, without responsibilities hanging over her head. I wonder how long it's been for me too, come to think of it.

Jack can barely hold us back as we push forward to get to the park. The two of us have some sort of tunnel vision. Finally, we get to a bench, and Jack unclips our leashes.

"Alright, you two. Go have fun, enjoy yourselves. The others should be here soon," Jack says.

"The others?" Brescia echoes. "Who else is coming?"

"I dunno, but…" I see something flying out of the corner of my eye and whip my head around to see it. "Ball! Brescia, look, ball!"

"Ball!" she replies enthusiastically. We both tear off in the direction of the ball, amidst five or six other dogs of various sizes. I overtake a Shih Tzu in my excitement, and soon a sheepdog with fur growing into his eyes barrels into me as well to get to the ball, yelling a 'sorry dude' back towards me. I can't help but laugh, causing me to almost trip and fall.

Brescia has quickly forgotten about the ball and is playing tug-of-war with a Doberman and a thick pink rope. She looks concentrated, focused on getting the rope from her opponent, but there's a sparkle in her eye that shows she's enjoying herself. She wins the first round, as I thought she would, but then they play again, and she lets the Doberman win. They say 'good game' and part ways. Brescia trots towards me, her eyes shining.

103

"That was *so much fun!*" she exclaims. "I've missed this."

"You looked like you were enjoying yourself," I replied. "You sure do play a mean game of tug-of-war." Brescia beams with pride as Jack walks over to us.

"You guys having fun?" he asks. I bark with excitement and run around in little circles. Brescia also barks with excitement, her tail wagging a mile a minute. Jack sticks his hand out to pet us, and Brescia closes her eyes and sighs with contentment.

"It feels like I've died and gone to doggy heaven," she says as Jack enthusiastically pets her back.

I hear a yell from behind us, and I can't quite figure out what the person is trying to say. Apparently Jack recognizes the voice, and he stands up. We look in the direction of where the yell came from and at first, the person waving is all we notice.

"Look who's here, guys!" Jack says.

"I don't know this person, who…" I trail off.

"MAMA! DADDY!"

Brescia looks as if she might pass out.

"Oh my… oh my goodness… Scar, it's…"

Ellie pulls at her leash so hard I think it might break. Finally, her owner bends down and takes it off. The second the leash is gone, Ellie bolts towards us.

"MAMA, DADDY, IT'S ME!" she yells.

"Hi! How's your new family?" I ask as Ellie runs around me and Brescia, round and round, until I get dizzy just watching her. She stops in front of us with a little skid.

"They're AWESOME!" she exclaims. "They have a POOL!"

"They do? That sounds amazing," says Brescia. "Are the humans treating you well?" she asks afterward, all concerned.

"Yes! Yep, yep," says Ellie. "The kids pet me *aaaaaaall* the time! They like to read me stories, and they put me in a little floaty thingy when we go to the pool. I don't think they know I can swim, but I like the floaty thingy. It's shiny! And pink!"

"I'm so glad you're happy, Ellie," I tell her. "Have you seen Dusty or Tina at all yet?"

"Dusty lives next door, and I see Tina when we go on our long walks, but not the short ones," Ellie explains. "Maybe they'll come here, and we can play together!!"

As if on cue, I hear a frantic yipping noise, and sure enough, Tina and Dusty have arrived. They, just like Ellie, barge over the second their leash is off. The pups tussle around in the dust, play fighting and teasing each other.

"There's no way you can pin me down – ack!" This comes from an overconfident Ellie, rolling around with Dusty.

"I'm gonna getcha, I'm gonna getcha…" teases Tina, who has pounced on Dusty and is chasing him around. Ellie is laughing so hard that she can't get up.

"It's amazing that we're all together again, even for such a small while," Brescia says.

"Mama, I missed you," says Dusty as he pins Ellie to the ground again, who is complaining and giggling at the same time.

"Why… How did you get so strong?" Ellie pouts, wriggling under her brother. "You're supposed to be younger than me!"

"Only by a few hours," Dusty replies, sticking out his tongue at her. Ellie sticks her tongue right back.

"We missed you too," says Brescia. "So, so much."

The pups stop tussling and all go to hug Brescia. I wish I could take a picture of this, to keep this memory forever. But instead, I settle for watching them so that the memory is ingrained in my brain forever. After they finish hugging their mom, they run to me (which isn't that long of a distance, so they end up bumping into one another as they try to stop just as fast as they started) and hug me too. My heart sings.

"It's so great to see you guys reunited," says a human whose name I don't know. "Ellie, why don't you invite your family to get some water? It's hot out today, and we wouldn't want you to overheat now, would you?"

"Come on, come on! These people have the BEST water!" Ellie scampers away to the water, and we all follow her. I hear a soft 'all water tastes the same, Ellie' from Tina, followed by Ellie blowing a big fat raspberry at her older sister. Tina giggles and blows one back. This brings about a thirty-second-long raspberry competition that Dusty joins into soon after. It ends when the water is brought out, and their attention immediately shifts.

The human who spoke earlier, who I assume is Ellie's owner, laughs seeing all the pups drinking out of the small bowl.

"There's enough water for everyone, there's no need to fight over it," she says with a small chuckle. It's clear as day that they're not fighting, just excited and a little hyper, but of course, the human wouldn't know that.

Jack brings out water for Brescia and me as well, and sets our bowl down alongside the pups'. As we drink, a small dog comes and starts drinking our water too. I don't notice the breed at first, but then learn it's the Shih Tzu from earlier.

"Bobby, come on now! Don't drink from other people's water bowls, you know this!" says his owner. "Terribly sorry, I swear I brought water, but he's a very social little guy and doesn't always understand personal space!"

"Don't worry about it," says Jack with a laugh. I stop drinking, and the Shih Tzu Bobby stops as well.

"Hi!" he says excitedly. "I'm Bobby!"

"I'm Scar," I reply. "Nice to meet you. This is my wife, Brescia, and these are our pups!" At the word 'pups', the trio stops drinking water and prances over to me. "This is Tina, Ellie, and Dusty!"

"Hey, little ones!" says Bobby excitedly. "Man, they're so lovely!"

"They definitely are," says Brescia. "We're very proud of them."

"Bobby, time to say goodbye to your new friends, we have to go now, I have a meeting," says Bobby's owner.

"Awh, damn. Well, it was great meeting you and your fam, have a good day!"

"Bye!" I reply, the pups all echoing various different versions of 'bye' until he's out of earshot.

Dusty's owner, a small boy who I think is actually Kate's nephew, not Jack's, holds out a new yellow tennis ball.

"Dusty, do you and your friends want to play?" asks the boy.

"How does he know your name?" I ask, bewildered.

"They don't! Just lucky that they picked the name, I guess," says Dusty, before jumping up and down excitedly at the sight of the ball. Ellie and Tina join, bouncing up and down. The boy throws the ball with all his might, giggling as the pups tear after it.

"I got it!"

"No, I got it!"

"Me! Me! Me! My ball!"

"Let go, it's mine!"

Brescia chuckles, shaking her head affectionately.

"You know, any doubt I've had about having the pups adopted is gone now. They're clearly very well cared for, and the fact that they live close by and have the opportunity to see each other every once in a while is amazing."

"The only thing that would make this even better is if Comet were here," I add. "She would have loved to be playing and tussling around with the pups."

"She would. She's gone through so much. I wish there was a way we could help her, but…" Brescia shrugs helplessly. "I don't think there's anything we can do now but hope."

The pups race back, chasing Tina, who has successfully gotten the ball. She obediently drops it in front of Kate's nephew and sits, waiting patiently for the ball to be thrown again. Ellie tries unsuccessfully to get in front of Tina and closer to the ball. I'm tempted to tell her that being behind her sister is actually better because once the ball is thrown, she'll be closer to it, but then decide not to. She'll figure it out, she's a smart pup. Most of the time, anyway.

Jack takes a Frisbee out of his backpack and motions to us.

"The little ones aren't the only ones who get to play. Come on, Max, Brownie, fetch!" Jack expertly flicks his wrist to throw the Frisbee. Brescia and I lock eyes once for a quick second as it flies.

"I'm going to beat you!" I yell, tearing off.

"Like hell you are!" Brescia retorts, following me. I can feel her on my heels. She jumps up and catches the Frisbee right at the perfect time, landing gracefully. I skid to a stop, out of breath from my sprint.

"Got it," she says smugly with the Frisbee in her mouth.

"I'll get it next time, just you wait!" I reply. Brescia rolls her eyes and trots back to Jack with the Frisbee in her mouth.

The next time the Frisbee is thrown, a freak gust of wind throws it off course, allowing me to change course much quicker than Brescia and grab the Frisbee just before it hits the ground.

"I told you I'd get it!" I exclaim excitedly, dropping the Frisbee and stepping on it proudly.

"It's the wind's fault. I would've gotten it if the wind didn't move it towards you, so that's not really fair."

"I think you're just being a sore loser," I tease. Brescia rolls her eyes at me, but with a grin on her face.

"Well, well, well, if it isn't two of my favourite dogs in the whole wide world," says a deep voice from beside us. I freeze. I know that voice almost as well as I know my own. I turn around and my heart soars.

"Darrell!" exclaims Brescia, running over to hug him.

"Darrell, my good man, how are you?" I ask.

"Oh, you wouldn't believe it. It's incredible," he says with adoration in his voice. "My owner is the kindest man around. You wouldn't think it by looking at him, but boy... he really knows how to make this old dog's life everything he ever dreamed it would be. He's fed me so many different flavours of kibble to find out my favourite. It took a few days, and I didn't even know *what* my favourite was until he fed me that turkey one... now he feeds it to me all the time!"

"We're so happy for you, Darrell, truly," says Brescia. "Did you get to do all the 'relaxing' you said you would?"

"Oh yeah, my owner's really fond of watching movies at night, especially the ones with the big explosions and the people that can fly and stuff," Darrell says. "We've watched one almost every night since I came over."

"That's amazing," I tell him. "Have you seen Wally much?"

"Not much, but I saw him yesterday. Enough about me, though, how are you and your folks? Are the pups here?"

"Yeah, they're here," I say, looking back towards them. They're racing after the tennis ball again, Ellie in the lead. "Dusty's owner – see the little boy with the green shirt there – is playing with them right now."

"Oh, they look so happy!" says Darrell. "Y'know, I know I'm old, but I look at them and feel years younger, like I could also run around with them and play fetch. But

I bet if I were to start running around like them, it'd quickly prove me wrong." Brescia chuckles.

"Would you like me to go get them? I'm sure they'd love to see ol' Uncle Darrell again."

"Let 'em play. They'll come on their own time, and if not, well, we're here every week, me and my owner. Even if I don't play like the lil' ones do, I can still meet other older dogs and make friends. My owner often ends up falling asleep on the bench. We got here some time ago, so…" Darrell looks up. "Yep. The man's definitely asleep."

The pups run towards us at that point.

"Uncle Darrell!" yells Dusty triumphantly. "Guys, look!"

"There go my favourite pups! Come on over!" Darrell's sparkle in his eyes grows as the pups rush to tell him all their stories… at the exact same time.

"And they have a pool…"

"We got to play with the ball!"

"My house is HUGE!"

"Hey, Fred, did you find some new friends?" says a voice even deeper than Darrell's. We look up, and it seems that Darrell's owner has woken up.

"Oh, yeah, he called me Fred," says Darrell. "I don't mind, really. He doesn't often call me that, it's just like, for official stuff, ya know? Mostly he calls me Sleepy or Big Boy. Sometimes Freddy."

"I remember you guys! From the shelter!" says Darrell's owner. "How are you?"

"Sorry, sir," says a woman behind us who I soon recognize as Ellie's owner. Ellie rubs against her legs, then gets lifted off the ground by her. "Are they bothering you? Did they wake you up?"

"Nah, don' worry about it, ma'am," he says cheerfully. "If ol' Fred here's found himself some friends, I don't mind them bein' around."

"Are you sure? I wouldn't want you to be overwhelmed if you're trying to rest," says Ellie's owner.

"If Fred's okay with it, I'm okay with it. Freddy, ol' boy, are you okay with these friends bein' here?"

Darrell nods enthusiastically and grins at his owner.

"I think that settles it! Say, ma'am, I recognize you from somewhere... did you used to work at..." The owners get to talking. Turns out they used to work at the same company some time ago. Ellie's owner sets her on the ground and the pups keep talking Darrell's ear off about all sorts of things.

"And my owners have the SOFTEST carpet!" Tina exclaims.

"Mine have SO MANY COOL TOYS!" says Dusty.

"Mine let me sleep in their bed, but their mom doesn't like it, but I do it anyway because it's funny!" This, of course, was Ellie.

"Well, I'm so happy for you guys. I'll tell y'all the same thing I told your parents, that I'm here almost every week, so you can come see Uncle Darrell whenever you're around this here dog park, alright?"

"We will, we will!"

"Hey, Dusty! Do you guys want the ball again?" asks Dusty's owner.

"BALL!" The pups exclaim. They tear away through the park as the tennis ball leaves the little boy's hand. He starts laughing and follows them away.

"It really doesn't take much for them to be happy, doesn't it," says Brescia. "I'm glad they still have their playfulness. If they'd lost that at this age, I don't think I would have forgiven myself."

"You gave them all the care and love you could, and then they got owners who are doing the same. You gotta give yourselves some credit, right?" says Darrell.

Brescia nods contentedly.

"How's Comet, where's she at?" asks Darrell. Upon seeing our expressions, his eyes widen. "Should I not have asked that?"

"No, no, it's alright. Just… she's still there at the shelter. They don't want her to be adopted just yet because remember she tried to bite that woman? They don't think she's ready for a family yet," I answer.

"She didn't take the news well when we told her we'd be leaving," Brescia adds solemnly.

"Oh, wow. I hope she's doing better. Maybe she has an owner now or somethin'," Darrell says softly.

"All we can do is hope," I murmur.

"Fred, buddy, I know you love your new friends, but I think it's time for us to head out now. I've got some work to do around the house before dinner time," says Darrell's owner, standing up off the bench and stretching. "Buh-bye, Fred's friends! We'll see you around later, maybe, okay?"

We all back away from Darrell and his owner. Before they leave, Darrell gives us all one last 'see you later' and heads off.

Brescia and I watch him leave for a little bit until he's out of sight behind lines of traffic.

"It sure was nice to see him again," I say softly.

"I'm glad he's doing alright. He deserves this," replies Brescia.

We stay at the park until the sun starts getting really hot, and everyone gets a little sluggish from the heat. Jack gives me and Brescia some more water before clipping our leashes back on. The pups, also tired out from the heat and all the running around, lap up some water and then lay down on the grass.

"I'm so happy we got to see you guys again," Brescia tells the pups. "I hope we'll see each other again soon."

"Very soon!" chirps Ellie. Brescia and I each give our pups little hugs and doggy kisses goodbye, and then we each go in our separate cars to our separate homes.

"These last few hours were amazing," says Brescia wistfully as we get back in the car.

"They sure were," I reply, looking out of the back window at the dog park. Apparently, everyone had the same idea of leaving when it got too hot.

When we get home, Jack turns the sprinkler on so we can jump around and cool down. Brescia immediately jumps in the little jets of water, squeaking happily when the cold water droplets hit her fur. It takes me a little more time to get the courage to go in the cold water. I would've gone in on my own – I swear I would have – but Brescia ended up shoving me into the spray before I could.

"You wouldn't have gone in otherwise," Brescia explains with a grin.

"I totally would've! I just wasn't ready."

"If you say so."

We spend the rest of the afternoon drying off in the shade under Jack's back deck, talking and napping at varying intervals.

"I wish every day were like this one," I mutter when I wake up from my third mini-nap. Brescia yawns and stretches.

"Me too."

I suddenly find myself being more excited for the coming days. I don't remember the last time I've felt this excited about the future. Living at the Den, there was excitement, of course, but most of it was overpowered by the daunting reality that comes from having to survive, meaning that fun was one of our lesser priorities.

"Scar, can I tell you something?" Brescia asks sleepily.

"Mhm?"

"I love you." I smile and curl up closer to my lovely wife.

"Love you too."

Chapter 10: Under The Stars

The rest of July went smoothly, as can be expected. It was hot, but we went swimming a lot in Ellie's owner's pool. The pups were getting much better at it, and didn't even have to be put on the floaty things anymore.

We also went to the dog park a lot. We bumped into Darrell quite a few times, and he was always so happy to see us. We also met one of Darrell's old rivals from his dog-fighting days, before he joined the Den. Brescia and I were worried that it would go sour, but turns out neither of them held a grudge since it's been so long.

There were still a lot of things Brescia and I had to get used to. For one, Jack had a job to go to. And I don't mean the shelter, I mean a real, 9-to-5, everyday job. A career, if you will. When Jack had first adopted me, all those years ago, he was fresh out of college, doing what part-time jobs he could. He would wear random t-shirts and jeans, and maybe a hoodie if it was cold.

I had forgotten about that aspect of Jack's life until he came downstairs one morning with a suit and tie, and he had a professional-looking bag where, it turns out, he kept his computer. (I saw it when I decided to go sniff the bag to see what he was doing with it. There was a lot of paper in there too that I was very careful not to tamper with.)

Brescia and I decided to follow him to the kitchen, where he sat down and sipped coffee at the dining room table, shoes off, suit on, and his bag was leaning against the chair he was sitting on. Our food bowls were full, and so was our water bowl. He nodded to us and kept drinking his coffee.

A bleary-eyed Kate wandered down the stairs, eyes half-closed.

"Morning. 'S there coffee?" she asked. "Rowan's still asleep, by the way."

"Of course, it's on the counter," said Jack, downing the last of his coffee. Soon, we heard a faint sound of crying, and Kate sighed.

"I'll get him," said Jack. "You get breakfast." He kissed his wife on the cheek as she poured herself what I knew was coffee, but what looked like muddy water. Once, someone (Jack, probably) spilled some on the ground, and he was running to make sure neither me nor Brescia got any. So either it tasted disgusting, or it was poisonous to us. I didn't wanna test that.

Jack arrived downstairs with a much calmer Rowan in tow. They sat him in a high chair and Kate slowly sipped coffee as she attempted to feed him.

Coffee and breakfast finished, Jack checked his watch and said goodbye to everyone. He got in the car and zoomed off. Brescia and I watched from the living room window as the car went down the suburban street and drove out of sight.

At this point, Brescia, Kate, Rowan and I were the only ones left in the house. We finished breakfast together, then decided to just sit on the little chairs near the big living room windows and watch the outside, see what was going on in everyone else's life.

I quickly grew fond of these calm mornings. At first, I thought I'd be bored, but in reality, it was valuable time for Brescia and I to be together and slowly start the day on our own terms, without worrying about anyone being un-derfed, sleep-deprived, upset from a nightmare, or anything else that we'd have had to deal with if we were at the Den.

I was also spending so much time being alone with my thoughts that I began to think a lot about Comet. I hadn't seen her since the shelter, and I wished I could. But with baby Rowan, and his parents being super busy, there didn't seem to be much time to go back to the shelter willy-nilly. Maybe she was adopted somewhere already. I missed her.

One Friday morning, Jack feeds us and sits at the dining room table as usual. Kate walks down, dragging a big bag in one hand, and holding Rowan with the other.

"Almost packed," she says. "Just need a couple more things. It'll all be ready by the time you get home tonight." Jack kisses his wife on the cheek and smiles.

"Don't stress! Foggy Lake isn't that far away. We'll be able to have a nice dinner before we leave," he replies.

"What's going on now?" Brescia asks me, looking up from her kibble.

"Not sure," I reply.

"Can you put the tent in the car before you leave, dear? I can't see myself needing it before we actually head out," says Kate.

"Yeah, sure babe, whatever you need." Jack notices us looking back and forth between them and laughs. "Max, Brownie, you guys are going to get to see the woods again! Be in nature and all that. We're going camping at the Foggy Lake National Park for the next two nights. You'll be good dogs, won't you?"

At this, he bends down and pets me, getting fur on his suit as he moves on to pet Brescia.

"Oh, who am I kidding, of course you're going to be good!" He stands up and brushes himself off before getting ready and finally heading off to work.

"Camping, huh?" Brescia's eyes are shining. "I haven't been camping in years... My old owner used to love it."

It shocks me a little bit to hear Brescia talk about her owner. She doesn't mention him often, if ever.

"He'd bring me along, and throw a stick in the water for me to catch and bring back. He'd feed me bits of hot dog, or burger, or whatever other meat he was cooking on the bonfire. I think he was trying to spend as much time out and about as he could before he got too old," she adds, a hint of nostalgia in her voice.

"I don't think I've ever been camping," I reply slowly. "I think... I think Jack used to consider it too much of a luxury." An image of Jack at his desk in his old apartment flashes in my head. I used to walk up to him and lay my head on his lap to comfort him when college got hard. He used to pet me without really saying much. I can't imagine that version of Jack willingly going off to spend time in the woods for a few nights.

Brescia nods in understanding.

Jack gets home that afternoon. Before we know it, everything and everyone is packed into the family car. Jack looks back at me, Brescia, and Rowan as we sit together in the back. I have the middle seat, and Brescia gets the window seat.

"Everyone ready?" Jack asks. Brescia and I bark once to answer, and Rowan lets out an excited squeal.

We drive through the city, with me in the middle seat and Brescia – the lucky one – sticking her head out of the window beside her. She looks kinda funny with her windswept fur, but I'm not going to tell her. She's having the time of her life.

We get out of the car after a couple hours and jump out onto a mixture of gravel, leaves, and dried pine needles. Being in the car for so long, it feels good to finally be able to smell the forest again. But it doesn't look anything like the Foggy Woods I'm used to. The Foggy Woods from my Den days was wild, untouched and untamed. This one looks both calmer, more inviting, safer, but at the same time it feels fake. Like if someone had the idea of a perfect woods and had done what they could to make that a reality.

Kate sits on the picnic bench and feeds Rowan while Jack takes a long, heavy bag out of the car trunk. As Brescia and I watch, the plastic blanket-looking stuff, along with some long bendy poles, turn into a tent. People are so creative. How do they come up with this?

Brescia does a quick lap of our campsite.

"It feels like the Den all over again, somehow," she tells me. "You know?"

"Sleeping in the woods, out under the stars, surrounded by bugs and all," I reply. "I get it."

"We don't have to hunt to survive here, which is a relief," she says with a sigh. "But I'd be lying if I said I didn't miss the life we had before."

Jack sets up our doggy beds outside. Something about the air being fresher. I don't know. I'll admit I stopped paying attention after I learned we could sleep outside. Even sleeping inside the Den, you could feel the winds and breezes from outside filtering through the broken wooden planks making up the Den's walls. In a way, this camping trip is starting to feel a little bit like returning to our old life.

Jack steps on a branch and breaks it. I flinch, an image whirling through my head of the early minutes of the Den destruction: smoke slowly floating up and the crackling of dry wood. I notice Brescia looking at me strangely, and I shake my head to rid myself of the memories, murmuring "I'm fine, I'm alright" to myself under my breath.

When the sun starts setting, Brescia and I lie down beside each other and look up at the night sky. It's a little cloudy, but the way the sky goes from light to dark is still noticeable. I can hear Jack and Kate's breaths coming evenly through the thin walls of the tent.

As the first cooler breeze of summer wafts through, Brescia leans closer to me.

"Look! You can see the stars now," she points out. I look up and sure enough, small sparkles erupt across the pitch-black sky.

I hadn't realised how much I missed the stars.

Suddenly a meteor flies across the sky, and my heart soars for a second before I close my eyes tight to make a wish. Jack used to tell me that you could make wishes on shooting stars. I think as hard as I can about the image of my family together. Comet happy, the pups being able to see their older sister, and all the other Den dogs I've loved being there for each other.

I think about it so hard that it feels real, and I can feel myself starting to smile. The image in my head is so sharp it might as well be a memory of yesterday. I can see Comet's head tilted back, and I can hear how she laughs. I can see the sparkles in Brescia's eyes, and the enthusiastic little bouncing that Ellie does sometimes. I let out a little laugh.

"It's a comet," murmurs Brescia softly from beside me. I can tell she's smiling just from hearing her voice, but it's still breaking the image in my head like a glass window shattering, and all I can see in my head now is darkness.

I close my eyes tight and try to get that scene back in my head again, but it's distant and blurry. My eyes open and I come back to reality, staring at the dried pine needles in front of me, Comet's laugh playing in my head but no visuals to go along with it.

"Scar?" Brescia asks, concerned. She sticks her paw out to touch mine, and I take a deep shuddering breath to stabilise myself. "Are you okay? Talk to me, what's going on?"

"I made a wish on that shooting star," I say softly. "The… the comet." Saying that word, even when it's not referring to my daughter, hurts, and I can't make eye contact with Brescia. I fear if I do, I'll see nothing but concern and pity.

"They say you shouldn't tell others what you've wished until it comes true, but… at least tell me what got you so distressed. Let me help you," Brescia replies, coming closer to me so that our sides touch. Her dark fur is still warm from the summer sun.

"I never believed the whole 'if you tell, it won't come true'," I reply with a sigh. "I wished that at some point, we'd all be together again. Me, you, the pups, Comet, and all of our loved ones, together." Brescia inhales sharply and holds her breath for a few seconds before letting it go.

"That's what I wished for too," she says. "But that sounds like a good memory. Why… what… what happened that would get you so upset?"

"It felt so real, Brescia. Almost like I could see and hear what was happening in my head, and even though it hasn't happened, or might never happen, it was as real to me as you are, sitting in front of me right now." Brescia gasps as I turn to make eye contact with her. I don't remember the last time I had called her by name to her face. I also don't remember the last time I truly looked into her amber eyes. It's like I'm falling in love with her all over again, and my heart does a slow roll in my chest.

"And then the illusion broke," I finish, breaking eye contact.

"Oh, Scar," says Brescia. "I'm sorry."

"It's not your fault," I reply. "I won't let you blame yourself for this."

Another comet shoots across the sky and I don't close my eyes this time to make the wish. I lean against Brescia and stare up at the sky, looking at the stars. The sky is clear and dark enough that we can see even further than just the stars, we can see galaxies.

If that first wish won't come true because I told it to Brescia, then this next one has to.

I wish we can all be reunited and happy. I wish our family will be as one again. I wish Brescia and I don't have to live with the Comet-shaped hole in our heart that the shelter ripped from us.

And if that's too similar to the first wish, I don't care. That's the only thing I want at the moment. I'll do anything... *anything*... to have it happen.

The longer I stare at the sky, the more tired I get. Soon my head droops and consciousness softly slips away, but not before I hear Brescia whisper a soft 'good night, Scar'.

The next morning fades in, and I can hear birds chirping and frogs croaking, and the steady rustle of humans waking up and getting ready for the day. In front of me is a small doggy bowl of kibble, and as I fully take in my surroundings, I notice Jack at Kate at our site's picnic table having breakfast, while Rowan sits in a stroller nearby.

Brescia is watching me, but in a way that doesn't feel creepy. There's love in her gaze.

"I didn't want to wake you," she says. "You looked so peaceful."

"No dreams," I reply. "No nightmares." Brescia nods in understanding with a soft, affectionate smile.

I finish eating, and Jack walks up to me with two leashes in hand. Brescia and I bow our heads obediently and Jack clips them onto our collars.

"Don't worry, you two, it's only until we get to the beach," he tells us. "Come on."

The early-morning dew is starting to evaporate and I can feel the dry grass and pine needles under my feet, and it feels normal instead of feeling uncomfortable. If I don't pay attention to the flashy colours of plastic tents and tarp surrounding me, I can almost pretend I'm back at the Den.

Brescia falls into step beside me, looking around at all the birds and the rays of sunlight filtering through the canopy above. We walk together in silence, admiring the new views and trying not to get our leashes tangled in the wheels of Rowan's stroller.

There are small bugs everywhere, blackflies and mosquitoes buzzing around our heads and ants underfoot. The air starts to warm up as the summer day goes on. All in all, it's enjoyable.

Another dog passes us, wagging his tail and saying hi. Unfortunately, he's a little too excited, and his owner has to reel him in.

"He's just saying hi, don't worry! He's friendly!" says the owner, and I can't help looking at the dog in front of me apologetically. He's a brown husky – rare, but it happens sometimes. He looks to be about Comet's age, by the looks of it. Maybe they would've been friends, once upon a different lifetime.

"Sorry, dude," says the new husky. "I don't see new dogs very often – I can't help getting excited!"

"Not from around here?" I ask. The husky shakes his head.

"Nah, but that makes the trip all the more fun!"

"Come on, Sparky, let's go!" says the owner. "Time to get going, let's not keep these people waiting."

"See you around, maybe?" says Sparky, trying to hold onto our conversation as his owner tugs his leash.

"Maybe!" I call back, but soon he's out of sight.

As the hike continues, I can feel myself starting to settle into survival mode again. I don't know exactly why, but I can feel myself start to be more aware of my surroundings the more I'm in the woods with Brescia by my side.

I see a squirrel out of the corner of my eye, and without even fully thinking it through, I start to cross the trail to find it. My eyes narrow and I can feel my muscles tensing.

For a moment, I can forget about Jack, Kate, and the clunky stroller beside me, and all I can think about is how we need to get food, because the Den has a lot of dogs relying on me and those of us who have been there the longest, and I can't let them down. The squirrel is just sitting there in plain sight, holding a small nut, unaware of what it has coming for it. As I get closer, I can feel a small restraint on my neck. Can't imagine why, though.

"Scar?"

Brescia's voice.

"Hey! Max! Cut it out. It's just a squirrel."

Jack's voice.

"Scar! Leave it."

Brescia's voice again, and the directness in her tone is what snaps me out of it.

"Leave the squirrel. We're okay now. We're out of the Den. We don't have to hoard food anymore - or hunt at all anymore, for that matter."

I look into Brescia's eyes and instead of pity, or condescension, I see empathy and understanding. We've been through too much, it's clear.

"I'm not even *hungry*," I tell her. "We just ate."

"I know, Scar. I know."

"Max! Enough, come on," says Jack, pulling a little bit on my leash. "We need to get to the beach in time for lunch. It's just a squirrel. It's not doing anything to you."

I turn to look at the squirrel for the last time and watch it scamper up a nearby tree, watching the woods and the trail, but not paying any special attention to me.

"Yeah," I say out loud, looking at Brescia. "It's just a squirrel."

I fall into step beside her as Jack and Kate, now satisfied, continue our hike.

The forest soon fades away and we find ourselves on a beach. It's a small beach with no lifeguards, but there are a few families scattered on the sand, sitting on various blankets. Jack and Kate get us set up a good distance from the lake, and fill small bowls of water for Brescia and I.

"Drink up, you guys, we've been on a long walk," says Kate.

Brescia drinks her water and lays down on the warm sand, rolling around. The sun reflects on her fur and makes it so shiny it's almost metallic. I try to join her, but realise that I don't like laying on the sand. It gets in my fur and it's irritating.

I go to the water and play around in the shallows, leaving Brescia to enjoy herself in the sand. There are small fish swimming away from me and little weeds floating around, getting stuck onto my fur and waving like the world's soppiest flag.

She joins me a little while later, and her fur floats up and rests on the top of the water. She notices it and laughs, but it's not entirely out of amusement.

"Remind you of anything?" Brescia asks me, and it finally comes to me after a couple seconds of confusion.

"Oh yeah, the bath you had at the shelter," I reply. I wasn't there, but Brescia and Comet tell the story often. Brescia wades further in the water to get close to me, leaving a trail of sand floating behind her as it washes off her fur.

"Yeah." She spins in a lazy circle and her fur spins out, making a swirl on the surface of Foggy Lake. "Without Comet to get me out, we wouldn't be here now. Interesting how life plays out."

My heart drops into my stomach but I try not to let it show. I miss Comet, but I know she's safe. I made a wish on that damn star and I'm going to keep up the hope that I'll see her again.

A ball flies over our heads and Brescia and I lock eyes before tearing after it without a second thought. Brescia quickly overtakes me and grabs the ball with her mouth, looking at me triumphantly.

As I see the pride in her eyes, I can't help but think (yet again) of how much I love her.

But there's another thought in my mind too. There's clearly been a lot that's changed over the years, but the thing that comes to mind now is how she hated the idea of living with humans again, and would have done anything to get away from them. But now she seems happy, cared for, and less stressed.

Brescia starts swimming towards the shore to hand the ball to Jack's outstretched arm.

"You're looking at me weird," she announces as she passes me.

"Just... thinking," I reply.

"About?"

I explain to her, and she sighs.

"Everything and everyone changes at some point, Scar. I'm not immune."

"If there's one thing that hasn't changed, it's that I'll always be there for you."

Brescia beams, and the ball sails over our heads again.

This life just keeps getting better and better.

CHAPTER 11: THE HEARTH

We go to sleep later that night with tired legs, full bellies, and fresh air in our lungs. I don't know why I'm so tired all of a sudden. At the Den, we'd be on the go all the time, staying up much later than normal to do night watch, or waking up at random hours of the day for all sorts of reasons. Not to mention the pups needed to be taken care of.

Maybe now that I know what a good night's rest feels like, I can allow myself to do more, to exert myself more because I know I can sleep well to refresh. Whatever the case, my heavy eyelids close before I have the time to think about anything else.

I wake up and don't recognize the memory. It might as well have been any other day: Oscar, Brescia and I are sitting outside the Den, and we're supposed to be on guard duty, but it's a random evening in spring. It's warmer than we're used to, and we've just had a great hunt. There's no real reason for us to be worrying about anything.

Brescia laughs and leans against Oscar, and they smile at each other, full of love. I look away for a little bit, filled with awkwardness, but that fades away as a whine and a whimper of pain cuts through the spring evening. I don't know how far it is, but it doesn't sound close. We have to strain to catch the noise, so I can't imagine any humans in our vicinity can hear what's going on.

Brescia sits up straight and looks around, her ears swivelling to catch the noise. There's a low voice shouting, but I can't make out what's going on.

"You guys coming?" asks Brescia as she stands up to go to the noise.

"You sure it's safe, Brescie?" says Oscar. He looks off to where the noise came from warily, but stands up anyway.

"Whether or not it's safe, someone's in danger!" she says, starting to walk off. I jump up and follow her. She looks at me gratefully and Oscar sighs before getting up too.

"You'd make a great Alpha one day, babe," says Oscar, and Brescia beams, standing a little straighter.

The source of the noise is a small dog, a little younger than me by about a year, a black Labrador. She's standing at the bottom of the front steps of a house, shaking with fear as a man stands in the doorway yelling at her. Behind the man is a crying teenage boy cradling his arm.

"Unacceptable!" the man yells. "How dare you! You don't bite people! You dumb dog!"

"I'm sorry," the black Lab says in a small voice, but the human only takes it as a whine, and shakes his fist.

"I gave you a home! I gave you food and water! Love! And this is how you treat us?"

"I... I..." stammers the Lab.

"George, grab me the gloves, the big rubber ones in the closet. I'm taking this one back, there's no way we're keeping her."

The teenage boy nods tearfully and darts back inside the house as the man looks at the trembling Lab in his yard with disdain and disgust.

Brescia, Oscar and I look at each other from behind the bushes that we've decided to hide behind.

"What a terrible man!" Brescia exclaims. "I'm going up to her."

"Brescia, no. Not yet. If that man sees you, things could go really bad for you – for all of us," says Oscar. Brescia looks at her *boyfriend with a pained expression, but she soon recognises that he has a point.*

"What are we going to do, we can't just leave her!"

"Guys! The kid's back," I announce. Brescia and Oscar stop arguing and crouch lower.

The kid returns with huge yellow rubber gloves that go up to the angry man's elbow and fades away into the shadows, but not before yelling something angrily that I can't quite figure out. The man closes the door behind him and pulls sharply on each glove so they snap back into place loudly and aggressively. It'd be almost comical if the moment weren't so serious. The man strides down the stairs purposefully, and the black Lab backs up, tripping over her paws. She can't seem to take her eyes off the huge lurking figure in front of her.

Soon enough, the black Lab falls off the curb and into the street. Luckily, it's not a busy street, so there aren't any cars that could pose her danger. Unluckily, she loses her balance just enough for the man to grab her and pick her up. She whines and whimpers, and the noise pierces through to my heart. I imagine it's the same feeling a human gets when they hear another human cry.

It's at this point, as she twists and writhes around in the man's arms, trying to bite him on whatever part she can reach (which isn't much), she notices me, Brescia, and Oscar sitting behind the bush, watching her. Her eyes widen as she notices us. Well… maybe not us necessarily. She's making direct eye contact with Brescia. Brescia's expression is firm, and she nods once.

The black Lab is forced to break eye contact as the man takes her around to a car parked in front of his house and opens the door. The man tries to block her way out of the car, but as soon as she is placed down in the back seat, she dives in between him and the car, landing awkwardly and wincing, but managing to get up and run as fast as she possibly can to the end of the street. I wonder if she's noticed she's run past us.

"Storm, get back here! Now! Get in the car!"

"I'm not going anywhere with you!" the dog, Storm, yells, and stands her ground, her claws showing clearly against the sidewalk.

The human seems to only hear barks and growls, and looks on furiously from the side of the car where he stands.

"You want to play it that way, you stupid dog? You're going to die out here alone, see if I care! Just know that if you decide to start crawling back home, I'm going to call the damn Animal Control on you, and we'll make sure that you don't ever bite another human being in your life, let alone a child. Do you understand me?"

Storm hesitates.

"You have two choices. You can come back here, and get in the car, and I'll bring you to the shelter so that you can be taught how to behave better around people, like a proper dog. Or you can leave, and you'll never be loved, housed, fed, and you'll likely die within a month."

Storm doesn't move.

"Storm, NOW!" The outburst makes the black Lab flinch.

"Hey. Hey, Storm," I whisper from the bushes. She looks at me briefly but for the most part, ignores me. She starts moving forward slowly, almost as if she's forcing her legs to move more than she actually wants to. As she approaches the bush where we're hiding, Brescia gets her attention, finally, and she freezes on the spot.

"If you want to go back to that man, and go to the shelter, it's your choice. But just know that there's a safe place for you, should you decide to leave him for good."

At this, Storm's eyes widen, and she darts into the bush with us.

"Fine! If that's how you want to play it," the man booms. "Maybe it's for the best." He then turns around and trudges back into the house, pulling off his ridiculous rubber gloves as he does. He slams the door behind him so hard we can feel the vibrations through the bush.

Brescia is the first to speak once the tension and adrenaline in all of us fades away.

"Storm, this is Scar, my boyfriend Oscar, and I'm Brescia. We run the Den – a shelter built by strays, for strays. Are you alright?"

"I'm… I'm alright. Thank you. My name's not actually Storm though," the black Lab says in a low voice. "It's…" Her small voice is barely audible.

"Trey?" I ask. "Nice to meet you."

"Trails, actually," she says a little louder. "But… I kinda like Trey. You can call me that if you want."

"Trey it is," I announce.

"Welcome to the family, Trey," says Oscar. One of the first things he's said in a while. Trey gives a small smile, relieved.

Suddenly there's a crackle, and I whip around to see the Den in flames. Somehow I know that I'm older now, and that this is a much more recent memory than I want. My vision zooms in and out onto various things that I don't want to see: Ellie frozen in fear, Brescia herding the pups around, and Comet, Trey, and M trying to get everyone out. And then I hear it: her final, fateful words.

"Just one last time, let's check that the Den's really and truly empty."

My heart sinks amidst the rising flames and smoke, and I know exactly what's coming. My vision zooms out, and I'm back in my body, with Brescia, the pups, and the majority of the Den, successfully evacuated. The crackling gets louder… realer. Closer. Harsher. Sharper.

"What in the world are they—" Brescia breaks herself off. "They might not make it!" She lets out a shaky shallow breath to stabilise herself.

"I'm sure they know what they're doing," I remember myself saying, but my mind is a whole whirlwind. "Comet's a smart girl."

"You're right," says Brescia. "Guess we just have to wait."

But oh, the wait is agonising. Every second feels like I'm living life through honey instead of air. I give an audible gasp as Comet leaves the Den just in time, followed by M and a bunch of other strays that didn't want to leave. There's only one dog missing: Trey. I hope against all hope that I'll be able to see her emerge among the smoke, a dark figure visible among the ever bright flame.

Comet stands a good distance away from the Den and looks behind her, and I can see the moment when she realises that Trey is still inside the Den. I don't know what happened there, and why she can't get out, but it can't be good.

I can't risk Comet going back in there, whatever happens.

There's a big crack from the woods, and all heads in my near vicinity turn to see a flaming tree crack and start to wobble.

Comet runs towards the Den. I don't know if she's seen the tree fall, but I can't lose her. I can't.

I can't.

"COMET, NO!" I yell. "LOOK!" She turns, and her eyes widen in fear and shock as the tree falls. I can't close my eyes. I know this is a dream at this point, but I can't close my eyes. I didn't close my eyes the first time, and I can't do it now. I'm frozen in place, forced to see how everything went down in painful detail.

Comet backs up slightly, watching the tree, and with the loudest crash, the tree comes down…

Another loud crackle shakes me awake, and I jump up, breathing hard and my chest tight. There's a bright light coming from the trees, cutting against the darkness, and before I can think, I'm shaking Brescia awake.

She wakes up slowly.

"Scar… what… it's the middle of the night…"

"The… the…" I pant, looking out at the fire, and as my vision starts to settle and get used to the night, I can see there are other lights in the woods: flashlights, phone lights, and the sky is lit up by stars.

We're fine. We're camping with Jack's family, and we're safe. It's… just a campfire. Someone's watching it, cooking marshmallows and sausages, judging by the smell wafting over.

I look back at Brescia, still breathing hard, but also a little embarrassed. She notices the fire and hears the crackling, and the way her ears and tail flick sharply back and forth, I can tell she's thinking about the same thing I was just seconds ago.

For a few seconds, there's no talking. Just mutual understanding without any words shared between us.

"God, Scar..." Brescia breathes eventually.

"It was a dream," I say. "Well... worse than that, I suppose. Do you remember when we first met Trey?"

Brescia nods, letting out an exhalation that sounds as if she'd been punched, all the air coming out of her lungs at once.

"I do," she says. "I remember for a few weeks after we met, we were inseparable. Or rather, she wouldn't be separated from me."

"Oscar surely didn't like that."

"Yeah, well... Alpha duty calls even over those we love sometimes."

We sit in silence for a little bit as the crickets chirp and the frogs croak in the night.

"Her mother was a stray, did she ever tell you that?" asks Brescia. "She had never lived around humans before, and she'd only been in the shelter for about two to three months before being adopted. She wasn't ready, and nobody knew. That kid on the doorstep? He just wanted to pet her. He got a little too excited and a little too close." Brescia shrugs and sighs as she remembers the conversation.

"She did. But... she'd only told me after the pups were born. She trusted you more than anyone else at the Den. I like to think she tolerated me for the first six months before you and I started getting close."

That gets a pained laugh out of Brescia.

"At least you guys ended up making friends," she says.

The adrenaline from my nightmarish startle is starting to wear off.

"Feeling better, Scar?" Brescia asks. I nod.

"Yeah. Thanks, by the way. For being there."

"Always will be." I look up at Brescia with a grateful smile.

135

"Come," she says, moving to the side of her doggy bed. "There's enough space for me on the other half. Lay down. No more nightmares will come to you tonight."

"If only I believed that."

"I'll keep them away. As Ellie would joke, I'll eat them up before they get a chance to get into your brain."

At that, I give a genuine laugh and snuggle close to Brescia. She wraps her strong body around me, as if like a warm, fuzzy shield.

"Deep breaths, Scar. Deep breaths. We're safe."

The next morning, Jack packs up the tent and everything else that we've brought and throws it in the car. I find myself excited to go back home. I can see the pups. I can have a little more freedom since I know the city better than I know this place.

Brescia and I slip into the car alongside a clearly tired-out Rowan. The wind, filled with smells of tree sap and pine needles, blows through the car, bringing nostalgia and comfort.

I don't even realise I've fallen asleep until Jack opens the car door, startling me awake. I stumble out of the car while Brescia lands delicately beside me and nuzzles my neck.

"Sleep well?" she asks in a teasing sort of voice.

"Yeah," I answer with a yawn. "Did I miss anything?"

"Not really. An eagle flew by, but that's about it."

We go inside, and it feels a little weird to be back home. It feels like the house has been empty for quite some time (which, I suppose it has been). The voices echo along the empty walls just a bit, but the more we're in the house, the less strange it seems, as if the house is being filled by more than just bodies: love, happiness, and warmth.

Kate opens the shoe closet, throwing her sandals off and helping Jack put all kinds of other things back into the house. I notice she's left the shoe closet door open, and I wander in out of curiosity.

And that's when I see Snuffie, laying on the floor, covered in dust.

I raise my eyebrows. I can't believe Jack still has it. I would have thought he'd thrown it out, but after all this time, him still having it warms my heart. After I left to be with the Den, he kept it as a memory of me, even if he didn't think I'd ever be back.

Should I bring it out of the closet? If I did, what would I do with it?

As I look at Snuffie, hidden in the dark corner, the response comes to me much easier than I thought it would.

I'm going to leave it there. I don't think I need Snuffie anymore. I have my own family now: dogs that I care for and spend time with. I'll still tell the Snuffie stories to my pups, but making new stories with my family is so much better than anything I could have come up with when I was younger. Jack can still have it as a memento of our earlier days together, but I think my time with Snuffie is coming to a close.

And you know what? I'm okay with that.

After lunch, Kate takes us on a walk. I watch as Kate puts Rowan in a stroller, gets all her belongings in a big purse, and clips on our leashes.

The neighbourhood is relatively quiet. Not many people are on the streets on a random weekday in the early afternoon. Yet today, there seems to be a lot more people than usual. Brescia walks very carefully so she doesn't get the leash caught in the wheels of the stroller, while at the same time being very vigilant about her surroundings. I'm wary too. I'm not used to having these many people on our noon walk. Morning and evening? Sure. But not in the middle of the day.

Kate gets a phone call a couple of minutes into the walk. She picks it up with a smile.

"Oh hey, Camryn! Nice to hear from you!"

Camryn is Jack's sister, and Ellie's adult owner. I can't hear what she's saying from all the way down here, but Kate seems pleased.

From what I can gather from their short conversation, Camryn invited us to their place for dinner and to have a chill, relaxing evening with the family after what must've been a busy couple days. Kate accepts the invitation wholeheartedly. Brescia and I look at each other with excitement. We get to see our pups again!

"DOGGY!" yells a kid from up ahead. Brescia flinches, looking towards the noise. My ears flick back and forth.

Soon, we see a mom up ahead with a kid who looks to be about three or four years old. The kid is pointing to me and Brescia, rushing to get all the words out of his mouth.

"Can I pet them, can I pet them, Mommy, please? Please, please…"

"You're going to have to ask the owner, honey," says the mom. Once we approach, the kid stops and looks up at Kate.

"Can I pet your dogs?"

I wonder what Kate will say. Surely she can see Brescia's tension. I think I'd be okay with it, I can feel myself relaxing, but Brescia isn't quite ready for it. Her eyes are squinted, and her ears are flat against the back of her head.

"You can pet the grey one," says Kate. "The other one's not quite used to new people yet." The kid beams, and I see that the mom was hoping Kate would say no.

The kid walks up to me and starts petting me, but he's not very good at it. He starts at my shoulder and pets down to my tail, then *back up again the same way*. My skin erupts with goosebumps and my fur being rubbed the wrong way (literally) is not necessarily painful, but definitely very uncomfortable.

"Don't bite him, Scar, don't bite him," Brescia murmurs from beside me.

"I'm not going to," I reply, but my fur being the wrong way is really starting to get on my nerves. Finally, I just shake myself off, trying to reach my back, so I can get my fur to flatten the right way. Brescia walks up to me once the kid backs off so she can help me. Soon, I am back to normal.

"Thank you!" says the kid, beaming as his mom grabs his hand and they leave.

The smell of grilling burgers hits me before the sight of Ellie's house does. Brescia closes her eyes and sniffs the air, and soon we start pulling on our leashes out of excitement.

"Hey now, slow down you two!" calls Jack affectionately. Kate laughs as she pushes Rowan's stroller behind us.

"You guys go on, don't worry about me," she says. "Let Max and Brownie see their pups." Jack shakes his head.

"We go together. We're a family."

I smile to myself as I remember how, two-and-a-half years ago, being at Jack's was the worst possible scenario. Now I'm back with him, but I have Brescia with me, and I know my pups are safe with his various other family members, and I'm cared for and loved in ways I didn't think were ever going to happen. I slow down, and so does Brescia. Soon, Jack is walking hand-in-hand with Kate once more, and we match their pace.

Jack and Kate let us off-leash once we get to Camryn's yard.

"DADDY!" exclaims Ellie once she sees us. She stumbles out of a kiddie pool and gets her fur full of freshly mown grass, but it doesn't seem to bother her.

"Hey, Ellie," says Brescia, trying to get a particularly large blob of wet grass to get off our daughter's fur.

"How was it, how was it?" she asks excitedly. Dusty and Tina wander over in a much more relaxed manner, and I can't help noticing how their fur is also wet, but they don't have wet grass stuck to them.

"It was a lot of fun," I answer. I hear the crackling of fire, and at first, I don't say anything. But then I snap out of it. It was just a campfire this time. We were safe. It *was* quite a fun camping trip, all things considered.

Brescia answers all the pups' questions, from "how many other dogs did you see" to "were there marshmallows" to "did you guys see a moose". I jump in occasionally to add details, and the pups hang onto our every word, intrigued by our adventurous little stories.

Dinner goes by without a hitch. We lay down in the sun, and get to gnaw on some nice bones. Apparently, there were ribs grilling too. The evening doesn't cool down that much, so Camryn turns on the sprinkler. Ellie bounces up and down in place next to me as she watches the set-up, and once Camryn gets out of the way, she runs at full speed into the little water sprays.

"Hey Ellie, how's the water?" Brescia calls.

"*Freezing*!" Ellie replies, getting a face full of it. She runs out of the sprinkler, sputtering but still full of excitement and joy.

"It's so hot. I bet I'll run in before you," Brescia teases.

"You can try!" I reply, jumping up and running full-force towards the sprinkler.

It is, indeed, freezing. But the look on Brescia's face as she bursts past me only to get hit with a temperature shock is all worth it.

We head home as the sun starts to dip behind the trees. Brescia and I stay in the living room in comfortable silence for a little bit.

"These past few days have been fun," she begins. "But I guess there's no denying that we still have a lot to get used to when it comes to being a house pet."

There's no force behind her words when she says, "house pet". It's more matter-of-fact, more steady. Less accusatory.

"Well, you can take the Den away from a dog, but you can't take it out of one," I say. "Or however that saying goes." Brescia snorts.

"Alright, Mr. Philosopher," she teases.

"Is it just me, though, or does it seem now that there's a little too much calm? Like, there was so much of… well… everything, back when we lived at the Den. Survival, stress, and all that. Now it seems that nothing's happening," I point out.

"I see where you're coming from, but…" Brescia seems hesitant. "Wouldn't it be nice, though? To live a calm life for once?" I wonder if she's nervous about what my response is going to be. I wonder how long she's been thinking about this, too.

Suddenly, my brain starts conjuring up new images of our future. Sitting in the sun, or by the fireplace together. Fresh chicken, or ham bones at the dinner table. Being petted by our owners, or later by Rowan as a young boy, and us as older dogs that have lived quite a full life.

"I wouldn't mind a calm life," I reply. "Less work, less stress... sounds like a great idea."

Brescia beams.

"Max! Brownie! Are you guys gonna watch a movie with us?" asks Kate, walking into the living room, holding a content Rowan, who had taken a quick nap in the shade after dinner, and was now making cute little noises of excitement.

Brescia and I look at each other.

"I don't see why not," she says. Kate doesn't wait for our reply or anything before sitting on the couch with Rowan on her lap. Jack joins us a few moments later. He kisses Kate, and for once, I don't feel awkward or uncomfortable. I look at Brescia with a smile, and she gets the hint, shimmying along the carpet so we can watch the movie while cuddling together.

The movie starts with light colours and delicate music, and what look like princesses. Rowan is intrigued and excited to watch the movie, but twenty minutes in, he decides to start crawling all over the couch. He's gotten better at that, and is no longer kicking Brescia and me in the face. After a couple of laps back and forth, he makes sure he's secure and stable on the couch before stretching his hand out to try to pet us.

Kate notices and pulls Rowan back.

"Silly, you're going to fall!" she says with a little giggle inserted into her Mom tone.

Rowan tries to crawl away to us again, and now Kate gets it. She sets Rowan down on the floor, and he crawls in between us. Brescia is a little startled at that, but she ends up moving a little farther away from me to give him space. Brescia and I entwine our tails together behind him, and as he lays on the floor, the calm, soothing music from the movie gets him to sleep.

Kate gets up from the couch, and at first, I'm confused. Then she grabs her phone from her bag in the entryway.

She kneels on the floor and points the phone camera at us.

The contrast between that first movie night and this one is so stark that it's hard to believe it's only been two weeks. Brescia and I have a small human baby laying down comfortably between us, the same human baby that weeks ago was waking us up in the middle of the night and accidentally kicking us in the head.

A light *click* sounds as the photo is taken, and Kate climbs back onto the couch to show Jack, who smiles and chuckles softly. We finish watching the movie without a problem. Rowan doesn't even wake up. Kate picks him up gently and brings him up to his bedroom, whispering 'good nights' to everyone.

I stretch out on the carpet as Jack gives me one last pat on the back before walking upstairs to his bedroom.

At this point, we would normally go over to our doggy beds – it's become a part of our nightly routine I've gotten used to. This time, however, we just lay down side by side on the carpet, snuggling as close to each other as we can get.

"I don't wanna go anywhere," Brescia says sleepily. "Even if it's just to another room. I'm tired."

"Sleep wherever you want then, love," I reply. Brescia's eyes close, and she's asleep in minutes.

I drift off to sleep soon after this, a paw draped gently across Brescia's shoulders. The muscles in them are relaxed, not tense. Brescia makes a little nondescript noise and snuggles in closer to me.

It's about three in the morning when I hear a wailing from upstairs. It's not as loud as it was before, but it's still loud enough that Brescia and I wake up, even though we're all the way downstairs.

"Just when I thought maybe we'd get another good night's rest," I joke, earning me a playful smack from Brescia. She stands up silently and makes her way upstairs.

"Wait, where are you going?" I ask. "Brescia!"

"Just follow me, come on!" she whispers back.

I follow her up the stairs to the room where Rowan sleeps. Kate is on her feet, drowsy and her eyes half-closed. Rowan is in his crib, crying.

"It's okay, Mama's coming…" says Kate, trying to make her voice sound soothing even though I bet she's too tired to properly function. Then she notices me and Brescia walk into the room. I'm hanging out closer to the door, since I still don't know what Brescia's trying to get at, but she's walked up to the crib and put her nose between the bars of it, watching Rowan toss and turn and cry. When he turns towards Brescia and notices her, his crying slowly turns into whimpering. He crawls over to her and starts gently petting her, or at least trying to. His mouth opens in a smile and I can see a small white tooth poking out.

Kate scoops up Rowan to comfort him, but now all his attention is focused on Brescia. Kate sits down on the ground with him, moving his hand to pet her.

Rowan loves Brescia. That much we have alike. I love watching the two of them get along. Within minutes, Rowan is asleep again. Brescia slowly moves back towards the door as Kate puts Rowan back in his crib. She whispers 'thank you' before going back to bed. I can hear Kate's steady breathing from the second I get to the stairs.

"How did you do that?" I ask Brescia on our way back to bed. She shrugs.

"I don't know, I guess I just realised he needed some comfort. Mother's intuition or something."

"Well, whatever it is, you were right."

Brescia doesn't seem to want praise. She curls up on the carpet and I curl up next to her.

"You know, I wonder what he's going to be like as he gets older," Brescia whispers. "I think he'll be a super kind, respectful boy, eager to learn and adventurous. But I guess we'll have to wait and see."

"I guess we will. And we'll love him all the same, no matter how he turns out to be," I reply. Brescia nods, then lets her head fall softly back onto the carpet.

"Good night, Scar."

"Night. Love you."

"…you…too…" Brescia is asleep.

I remember the first time that Brescia and I were sleeping like this, back at the Den. It was when we made it official that we were a family, Comet included. Comet. I wonder how she's doing. I hope she's alright. I miss her.

Missing her never really goes away. I might not be constantly thinking of her, but whenever I do, the same pang in my heart shows up. I hate how my most recent memory of her is her heartbroken sobs on the day Brescia and I got adopted. I close my eyes and shake my head. I have good memories of her. I won't let this one day take away from all the amazing times we've had together.

Like that first day, we were officially a family, when I took Brescia and Comet to see the sunrise. It was orange and pink, and it reflected off Foggy Lake. It was such a surreal, incredible, heart-warming moment. If I could do that one experience over again, I would have it be the same way it went the first time.

As I lay here reminiscing, I suddenly realise that thinking back about the Den doesn't hurt as much as it used to. Those years were great years, with everyone happy and more or less healthy, supported and loved and all sorts of other great things. Of course, there are still memories that bring back pain. I miss Trey. I bet I will always miss Trey until the day I die and get to see her again. I wonder if M and Maisie are doing okay. I *know* Darrell is living the life he always dreamed of.

I check the clock on the wall. It's three-fifteen in the morning. I still have a couple more hours to sleep. I wrap my paw around Brescia again and close my eyes.

CHAPTER 12: LEGACY

The summer came to a close peacefully. Our days might have felt like time loops sometimes, but that just made every new trip that much more special. We went to the beach. The humans stayed on the blanket where the sand didn't start yet, so Rowan could sit on the grass and watch bumblebees fly around. We went to the zoo and I got to talk to a wolf. Brescia made friends with a coyote named Jim.

Rowan loved us. We loved him. Jack and Kate were some of the kindest, most supportive, most understanding and patient owners we could ever have asked for.

The pups were growing and becoming much more independent. Dusty had outgrown his sisters and took any opportunity he could to tease his sisters about it. Both of them hated it. Ellie was still determined to beat him in a fight at some point, even if she knew she was likely to lose.

As the last weekend in August rolls around, Jack and Kate arrange another family meet-up at the dog park. The hot weather is dying down, and there's a nice breeze, which means that the park is full of dogs. We meet Darrell again. He hasn't changed much since last time, if anything, he's even happier and friendlier.

Dusty is the first to show up to the park (besides Brescia and I) and immediately finds Darrell.

"Whoa! Who is this fine gentleman?" Darrell asks with a grin upon first meeting him. Dusty returns the grin and starts laughing.

"Uncle Darrell, it's still me, it's Dusty!" he exclaims. "You remember me, don't you?"

"Of course I remember you! Last I saw you, you were a small pup. Not super small, but definitely small*er*." Darrell looks Dusty up and down. "Or am I just shrinking?" Dusty laughs again.

"No, I grown! Grew. Whatever the word is. I'm bigger!" he says with pride. "My sisters are all small compared to me now." He puffs out his chest, and it's that moment of his guard being let down that allows Ellie and Tina to run up and barrel him to the ground.

"We got you now!" Tina cheers. Ellie lays on top of Dusty, pinning him to the dust.

"Yeah! Girl Power!" she adds. "Hey, maybe one day we'll catch up, and we'll be like Mommy and Daddy, and any one of us girls can beat you any day!"

I start sputtering in shock and mild offence as Brescia bursts out laughing to the point that she has to lean on me for support.

"She's right," says Brescia between peals of laughter.

"I know she's right, but wow."

Darrell chuckles as he watches Dusty struggle to get both of his sisters off him.

"They've grown into such fine young dogs," he says. "When I was their age, I was nothing like them. None of the playfulness or innocence or maturity that they had."

"It wasn't your fault, Darrell," says Brescia. "Some owners just suck. Yours… well, they made you fight."

"I'm glad, though, that I've been able to see them grow up in a healthy, loving family. You were, and still are, great parents."

"Thanks, Darrell. Appreciate it, man. I'm honoured." Brescia tilts her head down, flattered and humble.

"Okay, this has been fun, but can you... please... get... off... ack..." Dusty complains from underneath his sisters.

"Admit it! Admit we won!" says Ellie. "Say it!"

"I can't... if you're... urk... crushing..."

"Ellie, Tina, loves, get off your brother," says Brescia. Tina hops off, but Ellie, the little mischievous one, stays on for a little bit. I'm willing to give her the benefit of the doubt that maybe she hasn't heard her mother, but Brescia isn't. She stands over the pups with a stern but kind look on her face.

"Ellie... get off your brother." Brescia's Mom Voice has turned on. Ellie stops trying to pin her brother down and turns to face her mother with an apologetic face.

"Mom, can you do that thing that you used to do when we were younger and wouldn't stop fighting? I'll get off, but I miss that a bit." Brescia's stern face softens and she nods. Ellie climbs off her brother and Brescia grabs Ellie by the scruff of her neck, carrying her around as Dusty gets to his feet, looking mortified that he was beaten in the fight. Ellie squeals excitedly.

"I'm flying! Dad, look!"

"I see, you are indeed flying," I reply with a smile. Brescia sets Ellie down and opens and closes her mouth slowly.

"It's not as easy anymore to hold you guys like that," she says. "My jaw needs a break."

"Hey, but I wanna fly too!" says Dusty.

"Come on then, Dusty. Mom's not the only parent around who can do that." Brescia grins, mouthing a silent 'thank you, I owe you one' that I brush off. I'm not just doing her a favour, I genuinely want Dusty to be happy and have the sensation of 'flying'. I grab my son by the scruff of his neck and trot around. Dusty erupts into giggles.

Tina never liked when either Brescia or I did that. She doesn't like heights very much, or not being able to have control over her surroundings. She gets that from her mom. My jaw also hurts a little from that, but it's alright. The pups had fun. That's what matters.

"Hey Dusty, you forgot to admit you won!" cries Ellie as her brother sits back down on the dust.

"That's not fair, it was two versus one!"

"You said you'd admit it!"

"Fine then. Ellie, you beat me. I'm sure it will never happen again."

Their mini-feud now officially over, they look around for the nearest human who's throwing a ball or Frisbee. The minute they see a flying toy, the three pups run off as fast as they can in that direction. Dusty quickly overtakes his sisters in his excitement.

Kate motions for Brescia and I to come get some water, so we say a little 'we'll be back' to Darrell before scampering off to get water. She then proceeds to take a ball out of her bag. It's bigger than can fit in any of our mouths, and it's mostly white but has black spots on it. Like if a Dalmatian was a ball.

She throws it as hard as she can, and before Brescia and I can think logically about how this ball is *massive*, we both tear after it as fast as we can. I'm surprised that I get to it first. So surprised, in fact, that when I try to jump on it to grab it, I miss so badly that my trajectory gets me flying into a nearby bush. Brescia laughs so hard that she has to stop and sit down. I love when Brescia laughs like that. I love it especially when I'm the one who makes her laugh, or the pups. It's a little embarrassing at first, but the sound of her laugh is enough for me to ignore the embarrassment.

I climb out of the bush and roll the ball towards a wheezing Brescia.

"I wish Kate filmed that or something. Then we could watch it and have an endless source of comedy."

"The pups will never let me live this down, so can we not tell them?" I ask.

"Too late, I think." The pups are next to Darrell again, watching me, and they seem to be having a competition who can mimic me better. I roll my eyes, but they *do* look funny.

When we get back to the rest of the group, I see something in the distance out of the corner of my eye. I turn my head to get a better look and I see four dogs. They're small, thin, and from what I can see, they don't have collars. I can't see their faces, so I don't know if I recognize them. They start approaching the dog park in a small pack.

"Who are they?" Brescia asks. She's now intrigued by what this new pack of dogs is doing. Once they get to the dog park, they immediately scan the owners. I can see now that they look scared and tired. It hits me that they look a lot like how I did when I was first a stray.

"Pebble, why'd you drag us here? There's no help for us here," says a small beagle.

The biggest-looking dog in the gang, an English Setter a little younger than me who I assume is Pebble, looks around frantically.

"Well, there's gotta be some food here, or water, or something," she says. "Maybe when the humans aren't looking…"

"Pebble, don't be ridiculous, the humans will call Animal Control on us if we steal from them, you know this," says a grumpy looking Boston Terrier. "We should just go back to where we came from."

"If we go back to where we came from, Austin, the Hounds are going to chase us off again, and we all know Harley's going to try to pick a fight with them. We can't afford to wait much longer for food, guys." Pebble looks desperate, and isn't making eye contact with the dogs around her. She sniffs the air and looks around, back and forth, not even seeing anything in her desperation.

A Golden Retriever with matted fur, torn off in some places, snorts and rolls his eyes.

"They can't hold off all that food forever, at some point they'll have to cave," he says in a deep voice.

Pebble sighs, pressing a paw to her forehead.

Brescia pokes me, alarmed.

"New strays!" she exclaims. "I'm going to go talk to them."

"I'm coming too, obviously," I tell her. "Darrell, you coming?"

Darrell nods, stands up with a little bit of difficulty, and follows Brescia and me to the group of four.

Pebble's eyes lock on us and her eyes widen. She gathers the group behind her and snarls at us. Harley, the trigger-happy Golden Retriever, has gritted teeth and every muscle is tense and bulging. I was never that strong. I'm sure Harley could've snapped me in half when I was first homeless. Brescia stops approaching once she notices their fear.

"Hey, there's no need for that," she says sympathetically. "You can trust us. We were once exactly like you."

Pebble looks Brescia up and down. Her eyes skip over me and Darrell, and she motions for her friends to come out from behind her.

"Who are you?" she asks. "Why should we trust you? If you used to be like us, why are you in collars?"

"House pets," sneers Harley. "Look at 'em. They're too friendly and too... healthy... to know what it's like to be one of us." He says the word 'healthy' like it's an insult.

"Harley... look. The grey one has a scar. On his eye." This is the Beagle.

"That doesn't mean anything, Rhea, it could've been an accident."

Pebble the English Setter. Rhea, a Beagle. Harley, a Golden Retriever. And Austin, the Boston Terrier. Got it. On the streets, you learn very quickly how to be good with names and breeds. I didn't think it'd still be useful, all this time later.

"Let's all calm down. I'm Brescia, this is my husband Scar, and our good friend Darrell is in the back. Have you guys ever heard of the Den?"

They look at each other, then back at us and shake their heads, confused.

"The Den was a…" Brescia pauses. "…a community of strays. We lived in a house on the outskirts."

"You mean the burnt one?" asks Austin dubiously. Brescia nods.

"It's been a wild few months," I say. "But I lived at the Den for… almost six years, I think… before the Den burnt down. Brescia here, even longer. Darrell… about the same as me. We know all the best places to find food in the city and woods, places to avoid, how to hunt and how to steal, and how to fight if you need it."

The young strays all look at us wide-eyed. Even the easily-angered Harley has calmed down.

"Now, why don't you tell us who you young folks are," says Darrell.

"I'm Pebble. Ex-hunting dog, I guess."

"Rhea. My owners were homeless too. They… don't take care of me anymore." I bet there's a story behind that, but I don't want to know. It's her story to tell, and we just met.

"Harley. Fighter."

"I was a fighter too," says Darrell softly. "It's a hard life. Ruins you. Don't let it. I learned that the hard way." Harley's eyes widen, newfound respect found for Darrell.

"Austin. I was abandoned."

"I used to think I was abandoned before I realised there was more to that story," I tell Austin. "It's nice to meet you guys. If I understand correctly, you are in need of food."

Pebble nods with relief. "You know where to find some?"

"Of course I do. Things you learn from the streets stay with you forever. If you go to that one alleyway on that one street with the big apartment with the saggy front steps... the brick one... they always have a big pile of food there," I tell her. A throwback to the alley I raided on that day before the storm. The day everything began, and life as I knew it was going to get so much better than I thought it would.

"What if the Hounds are there, Peb?" asks Austin.

"No... no, they don't live in that area... this guy's alley recommendation is the complete other way. It's worth a shot, and it's not far," says Pebble, mental calculations running a mile a minute through her head. I can see it in her eyes, the way they look at the ground while flitting back and forth quickly.

"Who are the Hounds?" I ask, out of sheer curiosity.

The new strays look at each other again.

"Group of big dogs. They're strong and vicious. They basically run the streets now," says Rhea.

It's my turn to exchange looks with Brescia and Darrell. We remember those days. The early days of the Den, when there were other gangs. Eventually, they joined us. We have no hard feelings towards them.

"It'll do you no good to be competing for space and food," says Brescia. "We know from experience."

"How did you do it then? How did you survive?" asks Pebble.

"We formed the Den, of course," Brescia replies.

"*You formed it*?" asks Harley in disbelief.

"Surprised?" I ask playfully. Harley rolls his eyes.

"How did…" Pebble seems to be rendered speechless.

"We were your age. We gathered and recruited as many strays as we could. We found the headquarters. Agreed upon a leader. Someone to organise us, lead us, keep us safe. At first, it was our old friend Oscar, then it was me. Scar came to the Den later than I did, but he was right by my side ever since. Though we have lost dogs either to dog snatchers—sorry, Animal Control—and many other worse things, we kept supporting one another in any way we could," explained Brescia. I held in a snort. This was a huge understatement. But the general idea was right.

Pebble has nothing to reply. Neither do any of her friends.

"Pebble, this is a good idea. Do you realise how much better we can survive if we work together?" Austin asks. Pebble is deep in thought.

"I guess we can try," she says. She sounds unsure.

"It'll be worth it in the end, I'm sure," I tell them. "Trust us. Please. You'll do a lot of good to a lot of other strays. Though we can't continue the Den because of us being now adopted, new strays like yourselves will need help."

Harley's stomach growls.

"Pebble, let's listen to this one and find food, for goodness' sake. Saggy stairs apartment, remember? We can figure out about this whole Den business later."

"Right… right!" she exclaims. "Brescia, right? Thank you. I can never thank you enough." Brescia puts her paw on Pebble's mouth gently.

"You don't need to. Support your friends and family. Do what you need to. Most of the dogs in this city who used to be strays know our names. If you need help, and we're not around, anyone who knows me or Scar will be glad to help," she says. Pebble's eyes well up with grateful tears, and she nods wordlessly.

"I will. I will! Bye! Thank you!" The small motley group runs off in the distance. I hope they do well. They seem like a good crowd.

Brescia takes a deep breath that shakes slightly as she exhales. I approach her and lay my head on her shoulder.

"Are you alright?" I ask.

"You saw something in them, didn't you?" she asks. I nod.

"They remind me of us when we were young and trying to figure out how to survive in this cruel world. How we've grown since then."

We watch Pebble, Rhea, Austin, and Harley until they are out of sight.

"MOM! DAD! BRESCIA, SCAR, IT'S ME! I FINALLY FOUND YOU!"

Brescia and I whip around and almost pass out. Running at full speed towards us is Comet.

PART 3: COMET

CHAPTER 13: THE VOLUNTEER

I hate everyone. I hate everything. I hate life. I hate myself. I hate being alone. I hate everything so, so much. I didn't think it was possible to hate anything more than Charlie, but here we are.

Willa's okay, I guess. She's trying too hard to become my friend, and I don't want her to be. She's well-behaved, and has never bitten anyone, so of course someone's going to sweep her up again, and I'll be left alone.

I eat. I sleep. I go on walks. But nothing seems to matter very much anymore. All I can think about is how much I miss my family, and how they must be so super happy out there with each other.

Willa sits by me whenever we eat. She thinks I don't notice, but I can see that she always has a furrow in her forehead when we talk. I think she's worried about me. She shouldn't be. I'm not sick, and I'm not in danger. I don't need her.

"I heard Mike talking earlier," she tells me a week and a half or so after Scar and Brescia leave. I raise my eyebrows.

"Wow," I reply sarcastically. "That's new."

"Yeah, you're right, that man *cannot* stop talking about private things out loud. But he'll never end up knowing how much we hear and understand," Willa agrees, ignoring my sarcasm as she always does. It's unfortunate really, how much she tries to become my friend. She'll find out all that effort is a waste of time soon enough. I don't reply to her. I know she wants to tell me what he's saying, but I'm not going to entertain her by saying the stupid expected 'what did he say?!?!'.

"I heard there's going to be a volunteer coming. Her name is Charlotte, and she's a college student."

"Oh, great. Just another human who's going to end up loving one of us too much and going to take that dog home. She probably won't come back after that."

"I think it's going to be really sweet that she's here," chides Willa. "Maybe she'll be the nicest human being you've ever met!"

I roll my eyes and huff.

"Yeah, like *that's* going to happen."

"Come on now, Comet, at least give her a chance."

"Sure."

Willa looks at me like she's going to reply, but then sighs and remains quiet. Good. The less I have to interact with her, the better. We're not friends, no matter what she thinks.

I finish eating and go sit in the quiet room alone. If I stay out in the common area, Willa's sure to be wanting to talk to me more. I can't let that happen.

Once I get into the quiet room, I take a deep, shaky breath. Alone with my thoughts, I can be myself without pushing everyone away. I miss my dad. I miss my mom. I miss my siblings. My lower lip trembles. I wish they were here.

I hear chatter coming from the common area, and I turn to see Willa talking with the other dogs. They're laughing and joking around. I wonder if they're laughing at me, mocking me in my moments of pain.

But I can't help walking towards the glass wall separating the quiet room from the common area. I can't help the twinge of regret in my stomach as I see everyone having fun. I wish I could have fun with them too.

No. You'll just end up making a friend. You don't need that right now. They'll just end up leaving you again.

Willa looks back at me and grins, but then her face falls. She motions with her head, inviting me over. I avoid eye contact and walk back to the other end of the room where she can't see me. I chance another glance, and Willa's already gone back to having fun with the other dogs.

Soon the door opens, and a girl walks in with Mike that I've never seen before. She has very blue eyes that I can see even through the glass, and she's wearing an oversized black t-shirt with a bunch of red designs on it. Maybe it's for some kind of band? I don't know. It almost looks like she's not wearing pants until I see that she has small black shorts under her shirt. She has black boots with a bit of a platform on them.

She looks like one of those punk girls I see on our walks sometimes, except her nails aren't painted, she has no makeup, and her hair is what looks like a natural brown colour. She doesn't even have jewellery. No necklace, rings, or any other accessories at all, for that matter.

"Hey everybody!" says Mike, his voice warping through the glass. "This is Charlotte, and she's going to be volunteering here at our lovely shelter! I want you all on your best behaviour, alright?"

College student. She probably just needs to be here so it'll look good on her resume or whatever. She doesn't actually care about us. Then she'll get a job and go back to whatever city she came from, and forget about all of us.

Charlotte laughs and kneels down in front of Willa.

"I don't care if they're on their best behaviour or not. I'm going to try to get to know each and every one of them. Isn't that right..." Charlotte looks at the name tag on Willa's collar. "Willa?"

Willa yips excitedly, granting her a gentle rub between the ears. Her eyes close and her mouth widens in a grin.

"So, Charlotte, I'll be helping you get to know the ropes a little bit, so to speak, and then you can do things on your own soon enough, alright?" says Mike. "If you want to follow me, I can show you all the dogs' documents."

I wonder what it says on my document. Probably something like 'Violent and unfriendly, not safe for kids, known to bite'. I bet she'll be so off-put by me that she'll ignore me. Then she'll be gone, and I won't have to worry about her anymore. Perfect.

Charlotte nods and stands up, then her eyes flit to me.

Oh, no. Oh, no. Oh, no.

"Say, Mike, who's that?" she asks.

No, no, no. Stop. No.

"That's Hunter. She's not in the best shape, and she's been known to bite new people. She likes the quiet room a lot more than any other dog I think we've ever had," says Mike.

"Oh, that's a shame. Does she just have trouble trusting others or…?"

"Well, she was a stray. We've had her here before, but then she ran away, and now she's back after… well, you know. You must've seen the news."

Charlotte's eyes widen.

"Oh, poor soul."

I don't need her pity. I growl at her and pace the quiet room in a circle, making sure all my teeth are visible. Especially the sharp ones.

"Come on, Charlotte. I bet you're excited, but you'll be back soon enough. There's just some routine stuff I gotta show you, and from there you're free to do whatever you want until your shift ends."

I bet she's excited to *leave*.

"Right, yes. Bye doggies, I'll be back!" She waves at us and leaves. The door closes behind her and there are a couple of seconds of silence.

I have opinions about her. I can't keep them in for too long. I exit the quiet room, and all eyes are suddenly on me.

"Yeah, go ahead and gawk. Tease me all you want about how 'the hermit has emerged' bla, bla, bla," I begin.

"No one was going to…" Willa begins, then drops it. "We're glad you've decided to join us." I snort and roll my eyes.

"Charlotte sounds great," says a mastiff in the corner. I haven't even bothered to learn his name, and he's been here longer than I have.

"She sounds fake, that's what she sounds," I retort. "I think she's just here for the fact that this looks good on paper. I don't think she actually cares about any of us."

"Maybe, maybe not," says a young chihuahua. "But at least she can pretend to like us while she's here. And if she treats us well, that's all that matters."

As much as I don't want to get attached to this human, something about the chihuahua's optimism is snaking its way into my heart. Maybe I'll give this human a chance. One week. That's it.

"Fine. I'll give this Charlotte girl one week, and then I'll decide what I truly think of her."

Willa grins.

"I'm proud of you, Comet. I'm sure you'll end up liking her. I already do."

That's because you're gullible and trust literally anyone who pets you, no matter what kind of person they are.

I intentionally don't tell her that.

Apparently it doesn't take that long to look over a bunch of documents because Charlotte re-enters the room, Mike right behind her. The door opening makes me jump, and I run back to the quiet room almost by instinct. I stay there

163

behind the glass, warily watching Charlotte and Mike. Willa sighs and shakes her head affectionately. I wish she didn't care so much about me.

"Oh no! Did I scare her?" asks Charlotte. She looks crestfallen. Something about her wide eyes and ridiculously innocent-looking face remind me of Ellie.

I don't want to be reminded of Ellie.

"Probably, but it's alright. She sees it's only you," says Mike.

I see it's her, I'm not stupid. I just don't want her there. But Charlotte now isn't looking at any of the other dogs in the room, who are all wanting her attention. She's looking at me with her arm outstretched.

"It's okay, I'm not going to hurt you," she says in a quiet voice. "You want to come out now?"

No.

Mike puts a hand on Charlotte's shoulder.

"Give her time. She'll get used to you, and soon she'll be her normal friendly self."

Charlotte's face goes neutral. I can't tell what she's feeling, and it's starting to scare me.

"You're right. It'll take time. But I'm determined to get her to come out of her shell," she says with resolve written all over her face.

Yeah. Good luck with that.

Charlotte starts giving attention to the other dogs in the shelter, and I can't help thinking how Dusty would have loved her gentle nature. I wish my brain would stop reminding me of my family members.

Part of me wants to go back out to get attention from Charlotte. Everyone looks so happy, and it pains me to think how I'm probably missing out on good times. But then I'm reminded of Scar and Brescia being so ruthlessly torn out of my life, and I remember why I'm avoiding everyone. A lump gathers in my throat and I go to the farthest corner of the room, where it's dark and I can't see anyone. There's a cat tower in the corner shielding me even more, and for once, the confined space is comforting instead of scary.

I hope the chance I give her proves that I'm right. Then, even if everyone else is discouraged, it won't hurt as much when she inevitably leaves, and I'll never have to see her stupid blue eyes and innocent attitude anymore.

The sun sets and Charlotte stands up, complaining about stiff knees. I want to snap at her to 'get used to it, you'll be here for a while' but I know she won't understand me.

She approaches the door of the quiet room and kneels down to look through the glass wall. We're far enough apart that her face against the glass isn't everything I can see. She's also far enough away from the glass that her breath doesn't fog it all up.

"Goodbye Hunter," she says softly. I can just hear her through the glass. "I'll see you tomorrow, okay?"

I love how she stupidly thinks tomorrow's going to change anything.

I bark at her, loudly and gruffly, so she can tell I'm not happy about this information. She gives me an under-standing nod and smile before waving at me on her way out. She waves to everyone else too before closing the door behind her. Mike stays behind. Strange.

"You guys were so nice to our new volunteer!" he says with a smile. "I'll get you all treats tomorrow. Maybe she'll be the one to give them to you, how does that sound?"

A cascade of excited yips and barks emerge from the group. I roll my eyes. I bet the way that Mike said 'you guys' excluded me. But I don't care. I don't want to be nice to her.

Once Mike is gone for the day, he locks the door and turns the lights down low. Not completely off, but lower. I emerge from the quiet room with a sigh of relief and crawl as far into my cage as I can without the claustrophobia settling in. Willa, predictably, settles down near me.

"You know, Comet, I didn't want to call you out in front of everyone, but you have to stop being so mean," she tells me. She notices my mouth hanging open indignantly and continues on without letting me speak. "I know you're hurting, but that doesn't allow you to be rude to everyone."

"I'm not being rude!" I protest. "I just don't need anyone, and everyone seems to believe that we're friends or whatever."

"If that's what you think," says Willa with a sigh, and I feel like she knows something about me that I don't, which is completely ridiculous. How could she know me better than I know myself?

"Just promise me you'll stop being mean to everyone, okay? Withdraw or whatever all you want, but don't make everyone else hurt too," she adds.

I take a couple of seconds to think about what Willa's telling me and realise that maybe, annoying as it is, she's right. I sigh. I wish she wasn't so *aware* of me all the time.

"I'll do my best. Now, can you *please* leave me alone?" Willa shakes her head and chuckles.

"I'll leave you alone, for now." I roll my eyes before laying my head down to rest on my paws. I watch her back as she goes to talk and hang out with the rest of the dogs before it's truly nighttime. I lay awake longer than I should. The room is deathly quiet, the only sounds are breathing and whatever mechanical mayhem is going on in the walls and ceiling.

The last picture I have in my head before I fall asleep is of Charlotte's fearless hand stretched out to welcome me.

The next day, Charlotte arrives bright and early to feed us breakfast. I don't notice it until the hand coming to feed me doesn't smell like Mike's *at all*. But to be honest, Charlotte's hand smells better. Cleaner.

She fills my food and water bowls without spilling anything and plops a treat right on top, like the cherry on top of a cake. I give her a stare, my face neutral, if anything a little annoyed. I want her to know I don't trust her.

Charlotte doesn't reach out her hand to pet me, but she does smile when she notices me looking at her.

"You're out of the quiet room, I see," she says. "I'm glad to see it."

Alright then.

I eat my food slowly, watching Charlotte feed everyone else. Mike is leaning against the doorway, watching her.

"You know your stuff," he says approvingly once she's done. "You volunteered before?"

"No, but I fostered a lot of dogs when I was younger. I love them. Every dog deserves a good home."

I'm tempted to laugh. Of course, she would think that way. Pathetic sentimental loser.

"Well, you're going to be a great asset while you're here. I'm sure the dogs will love you, even grumpy ol' Hunter here."

Charlotte looks at me. I show her just enough teeth to get the point across, and make a little growling noise.

"In time, hopefully," she says with a small smile.

"We have a person here who wants to adopt a dog, you wanna go meet them at the door?" asks Mike, jabbing a thumb in the general direction of the door.

"Yeah, sure, no problem," says Charlotte enthusiastically. She glances once back at me, but it's not long enough for me to decipher what she means by that.

Soon enough, there's a family at the door. A man and a woman, and two kids. One's about twelve and the other probably about nine. They're both boys.

"So here is where we keep our dogs," says Charlotte. "Mike has been here longer and knows more about their disposition than I do, I'll admit."

"We're just looking for a friendly, already-trained dog, not quite a puppy but not too old either, someone who will easily fit in with our lifestyle. The boys are both really busy, and my husband and I both work full-time," says the mom.

"Well…" Mike directs them towards the other side of the room from me, showing them various different dogs. I notice he doesn't show me at all.

"What about this one, Mom?" asks the older boy, pointing to my cage. I freeze. I don't want to live with them. I *won't* live with them.

"Hunter's not yet ready to live with a family," says Mike gently. "It's gonna take her some time to get her used to a house. She hasn't lived in a house in a very long time."

The dad wrinkles his nose.

"Yeah, we're not bringing a stray home, boys. Who knows what kinda diseases or whatever they picked up from the streets. Pick another one." The boys immediately lose interest. I know I shouldn't bite more humans, but this dad is getting on my nerves. Before I can properly calm myself down, Charlotte taps on the man's shoulder.

"She's really quite healthy, you'd be surprised. And I'm sure with a little love, she'd be very friendly as well." My eyes widen. Charlotte came to my rescue? Stood up for me? That's a first. Among humans anyway.

"Good to know, but no, thanks," says the mom. "I'm sure all your dogs are lovely, but she's not what we're looking for." Charlotte nods and fades away into the background.

What was that for?

I watch Charlotte more than anyone else in the room. She's very observant, popping in to help when necessary but otherwise just staying back to let Mike do his job, learning from him.

I can't believe she stood up for me like that. It doesn't seem real.

Finally, the family decides to adopt a chocolate lab. I didn't bother learning his name either, but that's okay. I don't care. And now he's gone, and I don't feel any pain about this. Perfect.

When the family is gone, Mike follows them out to help them sign paperwork and everything. Charlotte stays in the room. Inexplicably, the dog she chooses to interact with is me.

"They shouldn't have said those nasty things about you. Just because you used to be a stray doesn't mean you're a horrible dog. I think you're just scared. Scared and hurt and lonely. I can be your friend if you want," she says. I want to cry. Somehow her words, combined with the things she's done for me make me trust her even more than I trusted Willa. Charlotte's not like any human I've ever interacted with. What's happening to me?

I don't growl. I don't show her my teeth. I just lay there in my cage. Charlotte holds her hand out slowly and gently, and all affection I had for her flew out the window as I bare my teeth again and snarl. Charlotte nods.

"Too soon, sorry. You let me know when you're ready."

"CHARLOTTE!" calls Mike from the other room. "CAN YOU GRAB THE..." This is quickly followed by incomprehensible gibberish, but Charlotte seems to understand.

"COMING!" she calls back. "I'll see you later, Hunter, sweetheart, okay?" It's all I can do to keep myself together. Her oversize band t-shirt (this one with less red and more grey-scale colouring) flaps behind her like a cape. Her sneakers squeak on the floor just enough to be heard, but not enough to be annoying.

Sweetheart. Even with all the things I've done and the way that I am, she is still giving me more of a chance than I've given her.

"Comet, are you okay?" Willa asks from her cage, at the other end of the hallway. I find that I'm holding my breath, and I start breathing manually again.

"She called me *sweetheart*," I say, staring blankly at the floor in front of me, trying to comprehend everything that's going on.

Willa gives me a big smile with soft eyes.

"I know you've been pushing everyone away, but maybe, finally, there's someone here you can befriend. Someone you can trust."

"Who, you?" I ask. Willa starts laughing.

"I mean, I wouldn't *mind* being your friend, no matter what rough terms we started on. I was talking about Charlotte, silly."

I nod.

"Okay. Okay, yeah. I'll give it a shot, I guess."

"That's a start. A good one, at that."

"I'm sorry I was so mean to everyone. Especially you," I admit. "It's not... I wasn't myself."

"I get it. It's okay. I forgive you. I never had anything against you in the first place. Shall we start over?"

Maybe things will get better from this point on. I hope they do. Willa and I talk for as long as we can, and I end up falling asleep mid-sentence at what's probably some time around one in the morning. You can tell when it's past midnight because I can see the moon in the second half of the window instead of the first.

"Good night, Comet. Sweet dreams."

I mumble a 'good night' in return, even though I was probably so tired it was incomprehensible.

They say time heals all wounds. I didn't think it was true when Willa told me the first time, but I think I get it now. And while I may not be completely back to who I was before, I think I'm on my way there, and it feels good to be some semblance of my normal self again. I don't remember my final thought before sleep, but what I do remember is a warm feeling in my chest.

Chapter 14: A Breath of Fresh Air

After breakfast the next day, we go on a walk. It's the first time Charlotte will be coming with us on a walk, and I can tell she's a little nervous. After all, we're going out into the city, off the premises. She and Mike, and about fifteen of us dogs. On top of that, the weather is nice, so there's sure to be many people around us.

Mike bends down to clip my leash onto my collar. Lately, I hate going on walks. We often go by the dog park, and I hate seeing all the happy dogs playing with each other and with their owners. I hate knowing that one of those dogs could be Scar, or Brescia, or any one of the pups, and I'm not there with them. So whenever Mike gets our leashes on, I squirm, and I'm just generally difficult. I can't bite too much. I snap sometimes, but not enough to injure anyone.

But today seems to be different. I wriggle around as Mike tries to get my leash on, but then he's interrupted by none other than Charlotte herself.

"Here, let me try," she says.

"It's alright, she's just stubborn all the time nowadays," grunts Mike. Charlotte smiles, but her eyes seem very insisting.

"Mike, I know I'm only a volunteer, but this isn't a question. Let me try to get Hunter's leash on, I bet I can do it."

"If you're so confident, then, by all means." Mike drops the leash and walks off to put leashes on the other dogs.

Charlotte gets down on her knees and picks up the leash. I get a good look at her hands. She's wearing a ring on her thumb and her nails have a new coat of nail polish that I can smell, but the scent isn't very strong anymore. Her hands are smoother-looking and less callused than Mike's are. It takes me some time to realise she's looking directly at me while holding the leash, almost like asking permission.

I don't move, just stare at Charlotte. Why would she be asking permission? Normally, all the shelter workers just wrestle us into our leashes and collars if they have to.

"I'm going to put your leash on, okay?" she says.

I know it's not a choice for me. I have to go on this stupid walk. But the way Charlotte is being so patient with me is warming my heart, slowly but surely. I approach her and lower my head so she can get access to my collar easier through my thick fur. Charlotte clips on the leash so gently that I don't even notice it's on until she stands up, and the leash goes taut, attached to me and my collar.

Mike looks impressed once he notices that Charlotte got my leash on.

"You actually did it," he says. "Nice work, how'd you do it?"

"I guess she just needed someone to be patient and gentle with her, isn't that right, Hunter?" Charlotte and Mike look at me expectantly. I just walk once in a small circle as a reply.

"Alright, looks like we're ready," announces Mike. "Here, hand me Hunter's leash, so I can attach it to the communal leash."

I hate the communal leash. It was okay when I was walking with Scar, Brescia, and the rest of the dogs that I actually *knew*, but now that I'm surrounded by dogs I barely know, it makes me uncomfortable. Sometimes if I happen to be beside the bigger dogs, my claustrophobia slips back in, and it makes the walk even worse.

I wrap myself around Charlotte's legs, hoping she gets the message.

"Mike, can I walk her? Just me?" she asks. She catches on quicker than I thought she would, which surprises me a little.

"Whatever you want, I guess, makes life easier for me. Hunter seems to really like you, for some reason. I've never seen her bond with another human being like that in all the years I've known her," Mike points out.

"I don't know why, but I'm honoured," she replies. She kneels down and pats me gently between the ears. It relaxes me in a way I'm not used to, so I have to give myself a little shake once she's done.

Mike's words confuse me. I don't think I have any *bond* with Charlotte. She's just way nicer than Mike is, and therefore, objectively speaking, she's my favourite. But then again, there's something about her, like she's making an extra effort to get me to like her, that makes me want to have this bond with her that Mike's talking about. And that scares me.

She holds my leash with a firm but gentle grip, leaving the leash somewhat slack as well. Mike does a head count of all the dogs, and soon we are off. Charlotte and I are the last ones out of the shelter, closing the door behind us.

"You just follow us, Charlotte, alright? We'll go our regular route so you can learn where we go. You'll never be alone walking all of the dogs, but it helps to know where you're going, just in case," says Mike from up ahead.

"Will do!" she replies enthusiastically. We start walking down the road, Charlotte and I are keeping silent beside each other as we go. Her knee-length pink sundress brushes against my back.

I wonder if we're going to walk in silence for the whole trip. Mike hates when it's silent because he finds it awkward, so he says the most random things, from personal life updates to pointing out things on the street that we see all the time, just so that words are coming out of his mouth. I don't know which I prefer, awkward silence, or awkward chatter.

"Silence is weird, isn't it?" Charlotte muses aloud, and I feel like she can read my mind. "Sometimes it's awkward, but sometimes it's calming. You don't always need to talk to be comfortable."

I realise she's right just as Mike yells, "We're taking a left here!". Charlotte yells back an "Okay!" before settling comfortably into silence.

I want Charlotte to talk. With Mike, his random chattering gets annoying because it's so obvious he's talking just for the sake of it. But with Charlotte, her voice is almost melodic. I like listening to it. I suddenly remember that she's not going to be volunteering here forever, and it makes me sad.

"Hey now, don't be sad," Charlotte says. I must've been walking slower, or drooping somehow. "I can talk if you want me to."

That's not why I'm sad, but if she's going to talk, then that's good. I want to know things about her. I bet her life is cool.

"Where to start? Well, maybe I'll start with why I'm here in the first place. You probably think I'm just here because volunteering looks good on resumes and stuff, right? I'd think that way if I was a little grumpy dog like you." I almost bark at her in protest, but she continues on without waiting for my reaction. "I won't deny that it does, but that's not why I'm here. I love dogs, simple as that. And I love the idea that I can just help out at a dog shelter and be with dogs that need love and care, and I can be there for them."

I don't know what to think of that. There's no way she's just that good of a person that she's only here because she thinks — or knows — that shelter dogs need love, and she wants to be the one to give it to us. Humans aren't *that* great. There's gotta be some kind of underlying motive. And besides that, the fact that she didn't deny that it looks good on a resume… she's smart. She's honest. I didn't think people could be so kind, or even wanted to.

I find myself walking closer to Charlotte than when we started. She keeps talking to me, telling me what she's studying in college (Computer Science) what her family's like (older brother Jeremy, younger brother Kyle, and younger sister Quinn, and her parents are together for thirty years) and what her apartment is like (small, but cosy, and she has a balcony).

She seems to have her life together. A great family, a kind, optimistic, empathetic personality, and a plan for the future. How is it that me, who's a complete wreck, has managed to meet this angel of a human? Am I dreaming?

We come back to the shelter just as she starts telling me about one of her really good friends from back home. It almost makes me sad that our conversation for now is over, but there'll be other walks. I hope that Charlotte will be the one walking me for all of them.

She takes off my leash and lets me go back into the room with all our cages, telling me softly that she's going to help Mike with everyone else's leashes before getting us lunch. I watch her as she goes, already missing her, which is ridiculous since she's not going anywhere, really.

Willa is one of the first to have her leash off. She shakes out her fur and meanders over to me.

"You seemed to be enjoying yourself," she says. "Charlotte's grown on you, hasn't she?"

"Yeah, she has. I really like her, more than I thought I would," I reply. She's sitting on the ground, reaching left and right to unleash the rest of the dogs.

"That's good! You gave her the chance, and it worked!" Willa exclaims, bumping into me affectionately.

"We'll see where this goes, I guess," I say, but in the back of my mind I already know where it's going to go. I want her to be with us all the time. With me.

We eat lunch while Charlotte sits on the floor amidst all of us and talks to us, pets us, watches us. She's sitting farther from me than I'd like, so she can't reach me, but I can hear her, and I allow myself to get lost in her words and her stories.

Once everyone finishes their lunch, they get out of their cages and flock to Charlotte, which makes me realise I've barely even started my lunch. So I have to sit in my cage and watch all these dogs have fun with her, while I have to just sit here and eat.

Charlotte doesn't even seem to care that I'm being excluded. She's not making any effort to see how I'm doing, or if I need any pets or hugs or anything. Were all her words and what she did before only an act? Did she ever truly care about me? Maybe this was just a ruse to get me to like her. Maybe she was just trying to get on the grumpy dog's good side. There's no way a person like her could ever actually want to be friends with me. What was I thinking?

I moodily eat my lunch and stay in my cage (as far in as I can comfortably be). I'm not going to go out and make any effort to join them if they clearly don't want me around. Of course, Charlotte would rather be with the excitable, friendlier dogs. It's just normal human psychology, or whatever.

Willa motions for me to get out of my cage and join the group, but I shake my head. It's not worth it. I just managed to trust someone, and now they've gone and thrown it all away.

"Hunter, love, don't just stay there, come on over!" says Charlotte, reaching her hand out, and all of a sudden, I feel welcomed again. All the dogs are looking at me now, and I feel weirdly exposed.

I pick myself up off the floor and get closer to Charlotte. Is this real? Am I not dreaming?

She reaches her hand out closer to me and rests it delicately on my head. Her hand is warm but not clammy, which is good. I don't like when human sweat gets on my fur.

"Hey, I didn't want you to be left out," she says softly. "There are a lot of you guys here, and as a volunteer, I want to get to know everyone. And I can't give my attention to everyone at once, that would be too overwhelming, surely you understand."

I do understand. What I *don't* understand is why my brain decided to spiral like that. There's no way I'm...

Willa gasps, a soft 'oh' of recognition. I'm going to have to talk about that with her later.

"I love everyone here at this shelter. From the grumpiest to the furriest to the smallest," says Charlotte. I bet I'm the grumpiest one she's talking about. "But I can't always give everyone attention, that's impossible." She chuckles and shakes her head, and her hand slips quietly off my head. I nod. I don't know what to do now.

Willa sidles up to me.

"You were jealous, weren't you?" she asks. I whirl to face her, my face contorted into a 'what the heck' face.

"No! No, that's insane, why would..." I cut off my sentence just as Willa raises her eyebrows at me.

"As always, your powers of perception leave no room for error," I say in a monotonous voice. "Maybe I was a little jealous."

"There's no denying that you and her have a special connection. It's the type of connection you normally see right before a dog gets adopted, but since she's a volunteer, none of us know what's going to happen after this."

"What do you mean 'none of us'? Who's 'us'?" I ask.

"Well, everyone saw the two of you walking together. I don't think any dog here missed that key bit of information. We talked about it a bit during our walk."

"*You were talking about me?*"

"All good things, don't worry! Nobody has any ill will towards you, Comet. You're gonna have to understand that at one point or another."

I take a couple of deep breaths to steady myself.

"Right, right." Then another word from Willa's earlier point stands out in my mind. "What do you mean 'connection when a dog gets adopted'?"

"You know, when a human comes in to adopt someone, there's often a connection that happens. It's not instant, but sometimes it is, and then the both of you can't imagine adopting and living with anyone else. Happened to me when I went to live on the farm. The farmer's wife was such a lovely woman, I'd do anything to live with her again."

"Do you think Charlotte will adopt me?" I don't know what response I'm hoping for. I feel like I'm not going to like my response either way. If Charlotte does end up adopting me, I'm going to leave Willa, and potentially everyone else in my life, depending on where Charlotte lives. She could be far, far away, not even in Fog Lake City.

But if she doesn't… she'll leave in the end, and I'll never see her again. So I guess there are pros and cons to both. But the real question is: Which outweighs what on that pros and cons list?

"I don't know. None of us do. If she did and kept volunteering, what would you think?"

"I don't know. Willa, I don't know. I didn't think I was ready for this."

"Didn't?"

"I really like being around her. I think she'd make a great owner. Maybe if she adopted me, I wouldn't even mind that much. But what if I never see you or anyone I know ever again? I mean there's already very little chance I'll see my... you know, my family... but that doesn't mean I want the chances reduced to zero!"

"Maybe she lives in the area. There's no need to panic over nothing."

"This is most definitely not nothing, so of course I'm going to panic, Willa! Do you not get it?"

"Of course I get it," Willa says softly, bringing my rising panic down to just a little pit of worry in my stomach. "Don't get too hung up about it. I'm sure whatever happens in the end is going to be the right thing."

"I don't know what the right thing is anymore, Willa."

"Then leave it up to fate."

The evening comes, and I'm planning to do nothing but actually have a good relaxed sleep. Except Charlotte seems to have other ideas.

She comes and kneels next to my cage, reaching for me. I let her stroke my back as my eyes close. She starts whispering, and I wonder if she knows I can still hear her.

"I read your document. I know you've been here twice, and you've lost so much. Those who were close to you are gone and adopted. You're temperamental and unruly at times, one to be watched out for."

Did she *just* read my document? I thought she did that a while ago. Why is she saying all this now?

"But I don't think that document is accurate. I think you're just hurting and need someone to love and care for you. You've been nothing but good to me since I've come here. More or less, anyway."

Why is she saying this? What's her point? I was going to sleep, but now I'm invested in whatever suspenseful speech Charlotte's making here.

"I want to adopt you."

What? She's got to be joking, she's only known me for a day or two. There's no way she actually wants to... maybe I've fallen asleep. Maybe this is a dream. It feels a lot like a dream in that this isn't actually happening, and I also feel a little bit like I'm floating.

"I want to be there for you and give you the care and support you don't have here. You're special, Hunter. There's more to you than meets the eye, I'm sure of it. And I think with the right home, you'll grow to be happier."

Yeah, this is definitely a dream. I feel like if I walked forward, I would go straight through the bars of my cage. Heck, probably straight through Charlotte as well. I get up and...

Boop.

I hit the bars of my cage.

So this isn't a dream after all. I don't know what to think about that.

"But I don't want to have you be somewhere you don't want to be. I can do my best to support you here until you're ready."

What's this? A caring human who's *not* going to rush into things? Who's going to listen to what I need and not what she wants? Wow.

The weirdest thing is, I think I'm ready. I want to live with her. She's proven time and time again that she's reasonable and loving and responsible. I just don't know how to communicate this. Charlotte opens my cage so she can get a better look at me. I immediately crawl onto her knees and curl up. I know I'm probably too big for this, but Charlotte laughs out loud and wraps her arms around me.

"I love you, Hunter," she says, and my body instinctively stiffens at that name. She pets me until I relax again.

"I'm going to have to rename you, that's for sure. Never liked the name 'Hunter', in all honesty," she mutters to herself. *Finally*. I know this is a coincidence, but the relief that washes over me is undeniable. I don't think I could have found a more perfect owner.

She stands up and puts me back in my cage. She doesn't seem to want to leave, but Mike is standing in the doorway with the keys.

"I'm locking up soon, Charlotte. You'll see them tomorrow."

"I have that orientation thing tomorrow," she pouts. "I'll only be here in the morning."

"Still. The shelter is closing."

"Alright. Bye, everyone!" She stands up and leaves. Willa grins at me from across the room.

"Nice," she says.

"I can't wait. Honestly. But I'll be leaving you, and everybody else…"

"It's *okay*. I swear. We'll miss you, sure, but that's life. You need this. Probably more than any of the rest of us do."

"Maybe you're right, maybe not, but it helped anyway. Thanks, Willa."

"No problem. Good night, Comet."

The next morning, Charlotte signs the papers. She clips a leash on to my collar, but tears off my name tag. It feels refreshing to have my little tag broken in two pieces on the floor, one that says 'Hun', and the other that says 'ter'. I stare at it. Maybe there's some metaphor in that, but at the moment all I can think about is that I'll never be Hunter. Ever again. And that thought is comforting. I'm about to start a new life.

Charlotte lets me stay while she helps out with the other dogs. I say my goodbyes, including a very warm and encouraging embrace from Willa. The optimistic chihuahua from earlier even says goodbye, even though we never actually had an entire conversation. Her name was Lilly.

Finally, Charlotte leaves for lunch break, holding me in her arms. She's pretty strong because she's holding me, a rather large dog, in her arms as if it were as easy as holding Lilly.

Charlotte sets me in the front seat of her car and then proceeds to get into the driver's seat.

"I'm going home for lunch. I think there's an uncooked steak in my fridge. I was going to have that for dinner, but I can always get another steak if I want one. I bet we'll come home, and that steak will have your name written all over it. Which, by the way, I don't know what to call you. Give me some time, okay?"

Sounds fine to me! I lick her hand on the gear shift, and she giggles, wiping my saliva on her shirt.

Charlotte looks at the rug on the floor in the entryway of her apartment, which has a bunch of space patterns. I can't read the words, but Charlotte seems to be looking at them, reading them, deep in thought.

"'Comet'," she reads, making me instinctively turn towards her. Then she looks at me. "That sounds nice.

Comets are pretty. Do you want to be named Comet?" I jump around excitedly. I can't believe my luck.

"Alright then," she says. "Welcome home, Comet."

CHAPTER 15: SEPARATION

"Let me show you around," says Charlotte. "Here is the entryway." I follow her through the apartment as her voice floats around telling me where things are.

"This is the living room, and this is the dining room… and kitchen…and over here is my bedroom, and here is the bathroom… and look! We have a balcony too."

She opens the sliding mesh door to the balcony with a little bit of a struggle. It squeaks on its way and gets stuck a lot, but finally Charlotte manages to wrestle it open to a point where we can both comfortably fit through the doorway. She stands on the balcony and looks out. We can see Foggy Woods in the distance on one side, a sizable portion of it charred and black behind all the houses blocking our view. I don't want to look that way.

On the other side, we can see the city suburbs in the distance, with pretty houses that have gardens and playgrounds and pools. I wonder if that's where Scar and Brescia live now. I do, in fact, see a few dogs walking, but I can't distinguish who they are. For all I know, they could be actually cats, or raccoons, or whatever other random animal would be walking alongside humans on a city sidewalk.

"It's gorgeous, isn't it?" says Charlotte. "The fire part, admittedly, isn't, but looking at the nicely organised houses and the people's gardens looks so peaceful. When I'm out of college and have a good job, I hope to stay and live in Fog Lake City."

I mean, I guess it is kinda nice. All those people who can comfortably live their lives without wondering and worrying about survival, and they can actually enjoy life. They get to stay with their families and not be separated. What an amazing life they must have.

And then I realise that I'm not that different from them anymore. I can comfortably live, since I now have Charlotte taking care of me. While I was ripped from my family, at least we're all safe in our respective homes. I wonder if they miss me. I wonder if the pups miss me, or remember me at all.

"Come on, let's go back inside," says Charlotte after a few minutes. She lets me go inside first, then closes the door behind her, rattling and squeaking again. She sets down a dog bowl and puts some food in it, gets a water bowl, and throws a couple toys out onto the carpet in the living room.

"I hope you'll be comfortable here. I have my college orientation, and I really don't want to miss that, so I have to go now. I'll be back," she says. She puts on her shoes and stares at herself in the mirror, muttering something like 'eh, good enough'. She opens the door and I follow her outside. I want to see what her college looks like too. She's going to spend a lot of time there, and I want to make sure it's a good place.

Charlotte stops in the hallway and realises I'm with her.

"Uh – Comet, no," she says. "You can't come with me." She walks back, unlocks the apartment door, and stands in the entryway. "Come on, back to the apartment."

I follow her back. She's got to be joking, right? She's just gonna leave me here, alone?

"I can't take you to my college, silly," she tells me, bending down to pet me between the ears. "I know you want to come with me, but my college just isn't a good place to bring you right now."

I'll behave! I swear, I'll be a good dog. I won't even bark once, or try to bite any of Charlotte's future classmates. I sit down with a bit of a *thump* and sit up straight, hoping to give the impression of a very well-behaved dog.

"I know you'll probably be a very good dog, but I have to pay attention to my surroundings. It's a big college, lots of new space." Charlotte looks up at the clock and bites the inside of her cheek.

"I'm going to be late," she sighs. "Look, I'll be back before you know it. I won't be gone long."

My heart sinks. Charlotte stands up to go to the door, and before I can figure out why I'm doing this, I run in front of her to stop her leaving.

She can't leave. She can't. She needs to stay. I need her to stay.

Charlotte mutters something else under her breath that I can't quite pick up, even with my dog hearing. She goes back inside the house and opens the fridge, murmuring 'please, please, please' under her breath. A triumphant 'yes!' emerges soon after as she pulls a half-full peanut butter jar out of the fridge. She grabs one of the toys she threw on the floor and slathers it in peanut butter. The smell fills the apartment.

"Comet, this is for you, okay?" Charlotte sets the peanut buttery toy on the tile floor of the kitchen and sits with me for a few seconds. Then, once I'm fully engrossed in the toy, she slips away. I barely hear the door close.

And then it hits me that she's gone. She's gone, and I don't know when she'll be back. She said she wouldn't be gone long, but it already feels like she's gone forever, and I might never see her again. Why did she do this to me?

I finish the peanut butter (nothing can stop me from eating peanut butter, *nothing*) but then now that the peanut butter has been eaten, I'm left alone with my thoughts. I miss Charlotte. How long has she been gone? It feels like hours.

I start to explore the apartment. There's nothing else for me to do anyway.

The kitchen is pretty small. There are cabinets, but none that are mounted on the wall, they're all just on the floor bordering the kitchen. I wonder what's inside all these cabinets. I pick one at random and the smell of compost hits my nose. Normally, this wouldn't affect me. I've dug through enough compost outside as a stray. But the heat, combined with the small space and poor ventilation, make me stumble around to close the cabinet door, then leave me panting and gagging. I'm never opening up any other random cabinets in this house until I see Charlotte do it first.

Then I go to the dining room. There is a small circular table with peeling paint, and two chairs. One is covered in books of all sorts of thicknesses, but they all seem to have the same theme of music. The other is empty except for one faded beige pillow.

The living room has a couch that looks like it's missing one of its pillows. I then realise that the missing pillow is probably on the chair in the dining room. The couch is a dark brown colour and the cushions are fading as well. I wonder how long she's had that couch. Maybe it belonged to her family. It doesn't quite smell like Charlotte, though. There's a wooden table in front of the couch that is so small I can see over top of it. I could probably climb on it. I *would* probably climb on it, except it has a very visible splinter. I don't think I want that in my foot.

Charlotte's bedroom has dark grey painted walls, but you wouldn't see it unless you were really trying to figure out what colour her walls were. She's covered most of the wall space in a mixture of rock band posters and sci-fi artwork. She has a desk with a computer on it and a lamp, as well as a haphazard mix of papers on top of it. Her bed is pretty normal, I guess. She has a stuffed dog on it.

I climb onto Charlotte's bed and sniff her stuffed dog. I don't know if she's gonna allow this long-term, but she's not here now and can't tell me no. It smells like her, so I decide to lie down with it and take a small nap.

But I can't nap. Now that I've explored the whole apartment, my mind is buzzing again. I miss everyone. I'm alone again. I wonder how everyone is doing. I want to see them again. I wonder if Scar and Brescia are happy with Jack and Kate. I wonder if the humans are taking good care of the pups. If they don't, I won't hesitate to eat them. The humans, not the pups, of course.

Her computer beeps, and I jump awake and out of the bed. The stuffed dog falls on the floor. I pick it up and gently set it back .down onto the bed before leaving the bedroom and pacing the apartment.

I'm tempted to rip something. Maybe one of my toys? I go to the living room and find a random squeaky toy, which looks like a watermelon. I squeeze it a few times, and sure enough, it squeaks. I keep squeezing it repeatedly, faster and faster, and finally, it pops. The only squeaks it makes now is the sad squeak of rubber on the hot wooden floor, which is nowhere near as satisfying as it was before.

But to my surprise, the front door opens, and Charlotte walks in!

Charlotte's back! She's back, like she said she would be!

"Hi, Comet," she says lightly. "How do you like the apartment?" She then looks at the living room floor where the popped squeaky toy lies lifelessly, its watermelon-y eyes staring at me as if to say, 'why must you leave me here to suffer?'

Charlotte picks it up and goes to throw it out.

"It's fine, there'll be more toys." She washes her hands and then goes into her bedroom to flop backwards onto her bed.

"The orientation was nice," she says. "I met some of my classmates and one or two of my new teachers. The building is really nice!"

I notice she's wearing a new grey sweater. It smells different, not like Charlotte, but not like any smell I remember.

"Oh, you like my new sweater?" She stretches it out and points to the different letters and words on it. "Look: F, L, C, C. Fog Lake City College. That's where I'll be studying." She points to a place on her sleeve. "I want to embroider 'Computer Science' on this sleeve, since that's what I'll be studying. I can't embroider for the life of me, though. I can play guitar, I can type, but that's about as far as my fine motor skills go."

I didn't know new things had a specific 'new thing' smell. I suppose Charlie never kept his clothes clean enough to have it smell like new clothes, and I probably was never around humans who had new clothes long enough to recognize the smell.

Charlotte gives me a hug before going into the kitchen for a snack. I eat a little bit from my food bowl as she decides on a small bag of chips from one of the cabinets that I have not yet opened.

"I need a walk," she announces through a mouthful of chips. "Let's go."

Charlotte swallows her chips and chucks the crumpled up chip bag back in the cabinet.

"By the way, I got something for you," she says as she walks to the entryway. She rummages through her bag and pulls out a strip of fabric I don't recognise until she turns to me and holds it out to give me a better view. It's a new light blue collar. It has some silvery details, and it doesn't have that cheap sparkly feel to it.

"You like it?" she asks. "I tried to find something I thought would be comfortable." She rips off the tag with her bare hands and fits it around my neck. It fits perfectly. Charlotte really has an eye for these things.

"You look great," she tells me, then clips a leash (also brand new) onto my collar. "Come on, no use waiting here for much longer, let's go outside."

Charlotte grabs her bag, then heads out and locks the door behind her, my leash wrapped around her wrist. Then we go downstairs and out of the building.

I've never had the opportunity to just walk around, being able to see things casually instead of being hyper vigilant about my surroundings. I see a bunch of people walking their dogs, and when they want to say hi, this time I can actually say hi instead of ignoring them. I wonder how many dogs thought I was being rude, when in all seriousness I was just trying to survive.

At one point, we bump into another human walking their dog, or at least that's what I think it is until the other dog completely ignores me. At first, I'm confused, and then I spot a special kind of harness, and then realise that the dog is likely a guide dog. It must be awesome to have a purpose besides just being a house pet. I've never met any guide dogs before, but Mom — Brescia — has. She told me that they aren't actually on the job 100% of the time, and can get time to relax. I don't think I could ever be as smart as a guide dog. Honestly, I don't think I'm cut out to be any kind of dog with a job.

Charlotte and I walk in silence through small streets and bigger streets, and I'm fine to let her lead me to wherever she wants to go. Soon she stops and looks ahead of her. I stop too, wondering what's going on, and then I follow her gaze, and my heart falls into the acid of my stomach.

"I think we took a wrong turn," says Charlotte in a small voice. She pulls out her phone to try and find the way back, but the damage has been done.

The Den… or what remains of it… is *right there*.

Glimpses of memories float through my head. From screaming and sobbing sounds too loud for me to hear anything else, to light flashing, almost blinding me. I hear my name being called, and it sounds like Ellie's voice. Sweet, sweet Ellie, who never deserved such a harsh experience.

"Comet! Comet, come on, we gotta go. I found the way out."

I shake myself out, trying to get the memories out of my head. There's a lump in my throat, and I want nothing more than to see Scar, Brescia, and the pups again. Darrell, M, Maisie, Trey, everybody. I wish the past few weeks could just reset.

"Comet… get up, come on."

It's Charlotte, of course it is.

"The GPS says this way. I see where we took a wrong turn now. That house, though… I don't think that thing's ever getting rebuilt. Or maybe it will be, who knows." Charlotte nods in the direction of some parked construction vehicles. Of course. They're going to remove any trace of the Den and its ugliness. Why would they want something like that to make the town look bad?

Charlotte's desire to leave seems to have left her. She has a glint in her eye that I'm not sure I like, along with a mischievous smile.

"Wanna go check the place out? Before it's gone? Let's go see, come on."

I don't think there's anything I want less than to do that, except maybe total earthly destruction, but Charlotte pulls me along anyway. When she notices that I'm dragging my feet, she scoops me up and holds me against her.

"There's nothing to be afraid of, Comet, there's no fire anymore."

I'm not stupid. I know there's no fire. I'm not afraid. This place just brings back painful memories. If there was a way for me to communicate this to Charlotte, I would, but unfortunately, she doesn't speak dog, as much as I might like her to.

Charlotte sets me down next to the ashes of the Den. Everything is charred and black, but it's no longer wet from the firefighter hoses. I poke one of the burnt wood pieces with my claw, and it comes back dusted with a black powder. I wipe my claw on the grass hastily.

Looking back at the Den now, while I still feel the sharp ache of loss, I realise that I can see other memories now too. I can see a silhouette of the old Den, the way it used to look, over top of what is actually there, and it's almost sharper than the real view. I can see Dusty and the rest of the pups taking their first breaths. Scar and Brescia's 'wedding'. Trey recounting an inside joke, and a version of me from last year laughing so hard I'm *wheezing*. I can't believe how much I grew this past year. I can see Darrell trading Scar a mouldy boot when Scar didn't know it was mouldy. I personally wasn't there, but Darrell always tells that story.

I don't know how, but somehow in the little bit I've been here, the painful memories that sprung up on me, while still painful, are not my only memories of the Den anymore. Being forced to stay here, forced to see this place where I lost my home and my best friend, forced me also to remember the good times. I'm starting to wonder if Charlotte didn't lose her way after all.

"Crazy what happened here," she says, standing up and brushing the soot off her knees. "You think we're done now?"

I think so, strangely enough. I miss the Den, I miss my old life, of course I do, but life is different now. I'll get used to it. If not now, then later. Life happens. I'll work through it. I survived one storm (albeit with Scar's help) and I'll work through this one alongside Charlotte.

I'm ready to go home.

Charlotte tugs on my leash and I willingly follow her, the Den to my back. On our way back, Charlotte stops to buy me a Dylan's Hot Dog from a stand on the side of the road. I haven't had one in *years*.

Charlotte laughs, snaps a quick picture of me, then decides to buy herself one too, covered in a ridiculous amount of ketchup. I wonder if she can taste anything underneath the overwhelming mound of ketchup.

We walk home together in silence yet again, a comfortable silence. It feels great to be going somewhere I can call home, somewhere that I am safe around a human who actually genuinely cares about me and can be there for me when I need her.

But yet, there's a small part of me that wonders if I'll ever see my friends again. I don't want this to be the last time I ever see them. I'm still young, relatively speaking, and I don't want my last memories of them to be memories where they're leaving me. I don't want *their* last memories of me to be goodbyes.

Whatever happens will happen. I suppose I'll just have to wait. As long as I'm with Charlotte, I'll be a-okay.

Chapter 16: Cleaning Things Up

Charlotte had the next weekend off, and we spent it all together. We went to the beach, and I expected the water to be much colder than it was, however Charlotte was having a hard time getting used to the water. She ended up just throwing a stick for me to swim and catch.

But then Monday rolled around and Charlotte brought me with her when she went back to volunteer. I met up with Willa as she was in line with everybody else, waiting to get their weekly bath.

"So what's it like, living with Charlotte?" she asked me. "You seem… lighter. Calmer."

"It's really great, honestly. She's the best human anyone could possibly ask for."

"That's great to hear! I'm so proud of you, Comet. You gave her a chance, and it worked out better for you in the end."

"Yeah. To think I could still be here, in these cages…" At that, I shiver a little bit. "No offence, of course." Willa laughs.

"None taken. How's her apartment?"

"It's pretty small, but we deal with it. She's on the third floor, too, so we have to walk up a bunch of stairs to get there. After a long walk, my legs get *so* tired!"

"Has she taken you to the dog park yet?"

"Not yet. I don't know why, though. Maybe she doesn't trust me to be with a bunch of new dogs and humans yet? I wouldn't be surprised if that were the case."

"Is she busy? Does she leave the house a lot?"

I look down at the ground. I don't like it when she leaves, so she doesn't do it a lot. But I know, logically, that she has to go places that don't allow me to go with her, sometimes. The thought makes my skin crawl.

"She leaves sometimes," I start slowly. "I don't like it, and I don't know why. What's wrong with me, Willa? She's a human, and I'm not, so *clearly* I can't go everywhere with her. But even if I were human, I can't be with her forever, there are times when she has to go places without me. So what's going on?"

Willa shrugs and moves along in line. I follow her.

"I don't know why exactly, but I had a neighbour who had the same problem. He would *not* leave his owner's side. But I think he got over it at some point before I left. I didn't see him much, in all honesty, so I can't really tell you."

It's now Willa's turn to get her bath, and she climbs in the tub. Her long collie fur hangs on her now, darker than usual and sticking to her skin. She looks a little weird, but I can look past it. I'm sure I've probably looked worse.

"How have things been at the shelter since I've been gone?" I ask as Mike scrubs soap onto Willa's back.

"Basically the same. Quieter, maybe, but honestly not much." Silence ensues as Willa gets her bath. I honestly couldn't care less about the baths when I was getting them, but Willa seems to be enjoying it.

She steps out a few minutes later and goes underneath the automatic blow-dryer. Her fur gets poofy again in a couple of minutes.

All the dogs now washed, I follow everyone back to the room with all the cages. Charlotte stays for a little while longer before she has to go home. She calls me back towards her and clips a leash on my collar before prompting me to 'say goodbye, Comet!'. I say goodbye to everyone, which the humans probably only interpret as barking. There's a chorus of "Bye, Comet!" and "See you next time!" before Charlotte leads me back out to her car and opens the passenger door, so I can sit in the front seat.

Charlotte gets home and takes a big machine out of the closet that has a long cord attached to it. I bet that machine takes up her whole closet.

She feeds me, then leaves the kitchen as well as me wondering what on earth she took out that machine for. Then out of nowhere, a loud "VVVVVT" sound comes out of nowhere and I almost jump out of my fur. The only thoughts in my brain are simultaneously 'get away from that infernal noise' and 'must save Charlotte from that loud thing'. It's everything I can hear, it's loud, and it seems to echo and fill the small apartment space. I hate it.

I run into the living room to see what it is when I see that it's the machine from earlier. Charlotte is holding it, and it's going back and forth across the living room floor. She turns it off and the noise dies down, but it still echoes in my ears.

"It's just a vacuum, Comet. It's not going to hurt you. I just thought it'd be a good idea to clean the house a little bit," she says. I stare at the vacuum as hard as I can, as if I can destroy it with a single glance.

"You can keep eating, Comet, don't worry. I won't vacuum too close to you. You'll be okay."

It's not that I don't trust Charlotte, I don't trust the vacuum. I don't know what it does and why on *earth* it has to be so *loud*. I reluctantly go to the kitchen again to eat, but I almost choke on my kibble as it goes off again. I run back into the living room and jump on the vacuum, hoping against all hope that's going to stop it.

"Comet!" cries Charlotte, turning off the vacuum. Phew. "You can't be getting in the way of the vacuum like that, it can be dangerous!"

Dangerous? Why even use that machine if it's dangerous? I look at Charlotte, pleading for her to stop with the vacuum. Yet again, she understands, and sets the vacuum down on the floor, walking over to me.

"Hey now, Comet, I'm going to have to clean the house eventually. I don't have a broom, so this is my only option unless I want to pay someone, and that's too expensive. I'm sorry."

I clench my teeth together and stare at the vacuum as if it's my mortal enemy. Charlotte laughs and picks me up.

"Don't worry, this will all be over soon. For now…" She walks over to her room and sets me down on her bedroom floor. "I'll have to keep you here. I'll close the door so it'll mute the sound a little bit, and you'll be safe from the vacuum."

I thought I'd be fine with that. Anything to get away from the noise and the horrendous vacuum. But as soon as Charlotte closes her bedroom door, something's not right. Every one of my nerves is on edge and I have an urge to get out of that room. Forget the vacuum, forget the noise it makes, I have to get out of this room if it's the last thing I do.

The vacuum turns on, and while the noise is somewhat muted, it's still all I can hear. To make matters worse, Charlotte's dark grey room makes it seem smaller than it actually is. I start pacing in place, getting more and more tense, and finally, I go up to her wall and press myself up against it just to feel something besides this nervousness. I curl up on the floor, the aggressive "VVVVT" noise resounding like nothing I've ever heard before.

When the curling up isn't enough, I stand up and put my paws up on the wall, so I'm standing on only my two hind paws. I start to scratch the wall, over and over. I don't even know why I'm doing this, but everything seems to be getting to me and I can't think rationally anymore. At one point, I reach up and my claw grabs one of Charlotte's posters. I don't know if it's important or not, but as I bring my paw down, the poster rips with a satisfying and loud "KRSHH".

Something in me stirs as I see the shreds of the paper on the ground. How *dare* Charlotte leave me here in this small room as the noise from the vacuum resonates through the walls? How *dare* she leave me here *alone*?

I reach up to another poster, unfortunately hung just a little too close to the ground. I reach up and my claw snags against it. I tear it down and this time, the ripping sound is louder and more satisfying, but that comes with the click of two thumbtacks on the floor beside me. I push them away under Charlotte's desk and keep tearing up as many posters as I can reach, even jumping to get some, which makes the rips faster and louder. It feels satisfying, a little like revenge in a way.

I stand back and admire my masterpiece as I finally realise I can't reach any more posters. It looks like a wild beast came and made a mess, which I suppose describes perfectly what happened. There are also claw marks on the wall from when I missed some posters, and there is paint chipping and peeling, long scratch marks against the walls.

It's beautiful.

That's when I notice silence from outside. Charlotte must be done vacuuming. I start pawing at the door. Now that all the violence against posters is done, I feel trapped again, and fear starts tickling my brain, a threat looming in the back of my mind.

I need *out*. I need to get out, whatever it takes.

I paw at the door and whine. I don't want to be trapped, I don't! Charlotte, where are you? Get me out of here!

"Comet, I'll be there in a second, calm down! I'm just putting the vacuum away!" I hear footsteps, and I peer through the gap between the door and the wall, trying to see some light, some semblance of comfort.

Charlotte opens the door soon after and bends down to pet me.

"That wasn't so bad, was it now?"

Oh, it was bad. It was pretty bad.

Charlotte stands up a few minutes later and finally gets a good look at her wall. She gasps and tiptoes over, looking down at the floor.

"Comet, what have you done?" she asks, her voice tight as if she's trying to stay calm, and not cry. "I should have never left you here alone, what was I *thinking*?" I now realise her tight voice is not holding back tears, but anger.

"Why would you do this?" she asks me. I can't reply now. I was so mad at her for leaving me that I wanted to hurt her by ruining her room. I wanted to see the pain on her face. I wanted to have the sensation of "this is how it feels!". But now all I feel is regret.

"Do you understand how much I paid for this apartment? The posters are whatever, I can print them again, but the walls, Comet? Really?" Charlotte pinches the bridge of her nose and sits down heavily on her bed. "It's not like you're going to answer me. What am I thinking?" Charlotte stands up again and starts pacing her room. She picks up the thumbtacks from the floor and sets them on her desk, staring at them, then the wall, then the ripped posters, and finally, me.

I'm sitting there in the doorway, shocked and surprised and guilty. I don't want to meet Charlotte's eyes, so I look past her at the walls. The walls that I ruined. The dark paint, scratched off and revealing the white wall base underneath.

And suddenly, a new fear sets in. Is Charlotte going to take me back to the shelter? Is she going to not want a destructive monster like me in her house? Especially when she goes to college in a month or so?

Maybe I'm not meant to be a house pet. Maybe Charlotte was wrong to trust me. My heart sinks, but I can't bring myself to leave the room in case this will be the last time I'll be with her as my owner.

Charlotte picks up the poster remnants and makes a note of what types of posters they are so she knows what to reprint. Once that's done, she stuffs all the poster remnants into her trash bin under her desk. Then she stares at the wall again.

"Serves me right for keeping my posters so close to the floor," Charlotte mutters. "Lesson learned." Then she sighs again. "I'm going to make a call. Come on, Comet."

She's definitely calling the shelter. I know it. Mike's going to pick up the phone, and she'll say "hi, Mike, I don't want Comet anymore, she's not ready, I was wrong about her" or something along those lines. I brace myself for Mike's voice to come out of the phone, but instead it's...

"Hey, Linda? Hi, it's Charlotte from apartment 302, I'm sorry to bother you, but do you guys by any chance still have that grey paint from my room? Mhm. Yep. Yeah, sorry about that, I just need a touch-up, my dog scratched it. Yeah. Thanks, Linda, be there in a bit. Bye now."

Wait, what? I'm not going back to the shelter?

Charlotte sits down on her knees next to me, but doesn't reach to pet me. Maybe I'm going back to the shelter *after* she fixes her apartment.

"Linda is my landlord. I asked her to paint my room when I first moved in a few weeks ago, and she was okay with it. She has some extra paint, so I'm going to get it from her apartment room downstairs. I *don't* want you to come with me, okay?"

I understand. I hang my head in shame.

"I *will* be back. *Don't* ruin anything else while I'm gone, okay?"

I lay down on the ground and close my paws in front of me. I will lay here, and I will not go anywhere until she's back. I can do that at least, right? She's just going downstairs. She's *just going downstairs*. She *will be back*.

Charlotte stands up, pets me once, then leaves to go downstairs. I lay there, staring at the door. She'll be back. She'll be back. *She will be back.*

She's not back in a few minutes. Granted, she didn't specify how long she'd be out, but it seems like she's been gone for way longer than necessary. I wonder if this is how Scar felt when Jack told him that he'd be back.

No. Charlotte *will* be back. She said so.

So did Jack.

I whine softly. I wish my brain would just stop worrying all the time and *leave me alone*. I go find food and water. I go back and lay in the hallway. I'm tempted to rip up the carpet, but I force myself not to by shutting my eyes as tightly closed as they can get. I'm not asleep, but snippets of memories force themselves through my brain.

The smell of sweat from big scary dogs as I get shoved left and right into tiny dark spaces. The bumps of Charlie's truck on the uneven forest roads, if you could even call them that. Getting put in a small box without being able to get out because of pure terror. The pain and cold of being thrown into an alleyway. The swallowing, surrounding loneliness of being abandoned.

No. Shake yourself out of it. That was a long, long time ago, and that's not going to happen ever again. I shake my whole body as many times as I can before all the images are finally gone from my head and I can see the apartment clearly again.

Come back, Charlotte. Please.

The doorknob turns and Charlotte walks in with an older woman with blonde, shoulder-length hair. Charlotte holds a bucket with dried grey paint spilled over the sides, as well as another smaller jar with something I can't quite figure out. The older woman, who I assume is Linda, is holding a weird-looking tray and a paintbrush, as well as a garbage bag for some reason.

"So glad you could be here on a short notice," says Charlotte. "This is Comet. Comet, c'mere, say hi to Linda!" I get up slowly and approach Charlotte, looking warily at Linda like a toddler who doesn't quite trust her teacher yet.

Linda reaches her hand out, and I stiffen, but let her pet me. I don't need Charlotte more mad at me than she probably is.

"So this is the one who scratched your walls?" Charlotte purses her lips.

"Yeah. It's not completely her fault, though, I left her there alone." Linda raises her eyebrows but doesn't say anything.

"Alright, let's get painting. Keep the dog out of your room, though, or we're going to have a much bigger problem than we started with." Charlotte looks like she's struggling not to say something rude, but instead she just nods and grabs my collar, setting me in the living room. She leaves her bedroom door open, so I can still watch her.

"The scratches aren't so bad, you're lucky," says Linda, pouring paint in the weird-looking tray. Charlotte grabs the stuff in the small jar to make the walls smooth again (humans really do think of everything, wow). A few hours go by, in which we go on another walk, eat some food, and wait for the wall-smoothing thing to dry. Finally, once the wall is ready, they start repainting. It really does look like my scratching never happened, except you can still see that the wall there is devoid of posters. The paint smell is starting to float around the apartment, but Charlotte opens as many windows as she can to let some fresh air through, replacing the paint-smell air.

"Alright, we're done! Thank you so much, Linda, you're a lifesaver," says Charlotte with a smile.

"You're welcome, hun, just keep that Comet dog of yours out of trouble next time, y'know?" Charlotte laughs awkwardly and nods.

"You got it. Let me help you carry these things downstairs." She turns and looks at me with an eyebrow raised. I lay down on the carpet. I'll be good. I promise.

Charlotte and Linda leave, and I pace around the carpet for a little bit, 'round and 'round, until I'm starting to wear a small circle in the carpet. Then I lay back down and wait for Charlotte, my tail smacking the ground over and over again to alleviate my stress. Charlotte opens the door and I jump up with excitement. She's back!

She goes over to the kitchen to get water and I follow her. She doesn't even say 'hi' to me. Is something wrong? Is she getting herself ready to take me back to the shelter again?

Once she finishes her water and sets it back on the counter, her face brightens up. She sits at the table and motions for me to approach. I lay my head on her lap, ready for the fateful words.

"We got a lot of work to do, you and me," she begins. "But you deserve a home just as much as the next dog. I'll do whatever work it takes for us to live together in peace, okay?"

I let out a sad little whine. I wish it wasn't so difficult for me. How did Scar and everyone else adjust so easily, and I'm making life hard by scratching paint off my owner's walls?

Charlotte kisses the top of my head and cups my head in her hands, giving it a little friendly shake. My ears flop left and right, making her laugh. I like making her laugh.

"Don't worry. I've got your back. We'll figure everything out together. But you got to make an effort too, okay?"

I bark once in acknowledgement. She's not mad at me! She's not taking me back to the shelter! She still loves me! This is amazing!

Charlotte opens the balcony door to air out the apartment, and I look towards the suburban area, seeing kids and dogs and other humans playing together happily. Charlotte breathes in the fresh air and sighs contentedly. I close my eyes and breathe in the fresh air as well. It smells like the city: exhaust and metal. Charlotte probably doesn't notice. Human noses are pathetic.

We stay out on the balcony for dinner and I risk looking at the charred woods, only to notice that I can't see as much of it anymore. I realise they're removing trees to make room for the new growth later.

One big charcoal trunk falls to the ground. I hear it land with a muffled "boom".

The earth rumbles for a second, and then all is calm.

CHAPTER 17: ONE OF US

A few days later, Charlotte gets a call.

She gets off the call with a huge grin on her face and a spring in her step. She picks me up and spins around a little bit.

"Comet, we're invited to my family's home for a barbecue! Isn't that exciting?"

I've never been to a barbecue. I don't really know much about it except the fact that there's good food. Hot dogs and hamburgers, and sometimes even steak! My tail starts wagging back and forth faster than I remember it wagging in a long time. Charlotte giggles and puts me down. My tail is probably starting to tickle her bare arms.

"Come on, we'll be gone for the weekend, so we should pack," she says, grabbing a big bag out of her closet. She throws in clothes, a water bottle, what I assume is sunscreen, and a bunch of my things as well until the bag gets so heavy she has to struggle to pick it up and sling it across her shoulder. She slips her phone, wallet, and keys into her pocket.

The packing takes about a half an hour, fueled by excitement and enthusiasm. She moves so fast around the apartment, murmuring things to herself so she won't forget them as she packs, and listing things on her fingers in a hasty whisper.

Soon, we're ready to head out. Charlotte locks the door with a decisive *click* and then heads to the elevator. I've never been in an elevator before. Scar says it makes your stomach feel weird. Still, I follow Charlotte into the elevator. It's really small, or at least smaller than I thought it'd be. The thick metal door shuts on us, and I can feel a sense of unease settling in. Luckily, we're only on the third floor, so we're out of the elevator pretty quickly. Scar's right, it does feel weird. It takes a few minutes for me to stop feeling like I left my stomach there on the third floor.

We get into Charlotte's car, and she throws her stuff into the backseat while letting me climb up into the front. We start driving. The window is open, and the weather is great, so Charlotte lets me stick my head out of the window when there's space. I never realised how many cars there are on the small streets of Fog Lake City, especially when the weather is nice. It was nearly impossible to stick my head out the window, no matter how much I wanted to.

Finally, we get to the highway. Charlotte closes the windows and turns the AC up all the way. I'm a little nervous about going on the highway. Charlie never went on the highways (then again, he also only owned a decrepit truck, which probably wouldn't even be able to drive at the speeds that the highway required). But the second Charlotte begins speeding up, my heart starts racing as everything else speeds by us. Trees, rivers, road signs, and other cars are all just blurs in my peripheral vision.

But soon I get used to it. Charlotte puts on some music in the car and makes sure to stop every once in a while so I can rest and get some water. I'll admit it's weird being back on the ground after driving so fast. I feel like my entire body has slowed down.

On our last leg of the journey, Charlotte opens the window for me again. At first glance, this place seems much smaller than Fog Lake City. The houses look a little older and vintage than the houses back home, too. When I stick my head out of the window, the smell of flowers and herbs fill the air. I can't even smell the car exhaust, or the harsh rusted metal smell. I was so used to Fog Lake City, I didn't know that there were other cities that could smell so nice.

Charlotte takes a big breath and sighs.

"Fog Lake City has one of the best universities around, and I'll enjoy being there for the next four years, but coming home to Basil Hills is always so comforting."

Basil Hills must be the name of this new town. I look out the window, mesmerised by how clean this town looks and how neat everyone's gardens are. Basil Hills is definitely the right name for this place. It smells floral and savoury at the same time, and the roads are definitely very hilly.

But the main thing that surprises me is how little street dogs there are. All the dogs and cats I see are happy with their owners, basking in the sun or playing in the sprinklers. Brescia got scratched by a cat once, so she doesn't like them very much. But I think they live great lives: they're cared for and able to sleep for so many hours a day without a care in the world. I wish I could sleep as long as a cat, but nightmares kind of ruin that for me.

We pull into a driveway and I get a good look at the house. There are ravens on the stair railings instead of the normal bulbs or weird teardrop-looking shapes. An older woman that looks like how I assume Charlotte would look at fifty opens the door with a grin.

Charlotte opens her door and jumps out of the car to go hug the woman, leaving her car door open. I don't want to be shut inside the car, so I climb over the controls and crawl out of the car through Charlotte's side, the breeze ruffling my fur.

"And this must be Comet!" says the older woman as she sees me emerge from behind the car. "She's beautiful, Charlotte, you made a good choice."

"CHAR-CHAR!" yells a boy's voice from an upstairs window. "NICE DOG!"

"YOU WANNA COME SEE HER?" Charlotte yells back. "SHE DOESN'T BITE!"

Yes, she does. She *did*, technically, but she won't.

The boy bounds downstairs and out of the door.

"Comet, meet my older brother Jeremy," says Charlotte. The boy, Jeremy, kneels down and shows me a ball. My ears immediately prick up in confusion. Why does he have a ball?

He throws it lightly over my head and for some reason, I tear after it, almost getting stuck in a rose bush. That would have hurt.

"Where are Quinn and Kyle? And where's Dad?" asks Charlotte as Jeremy brings me to the backyard to play more. The last thing I hear before I turn the corner of the house is 'they'll be back, just went to pick up a few…'.

Jeremy at first gave me the impression of someone careless and reckless — what with the bounding downstairs and the yelling from the window — but he's actually just a very friendly guy with a lot of energy. He showed me how to play tug of war, and I won! I was so proud of myself that I fell on my side in the grass and began rolling around. The grass here is so soft. I don't think I would have found grass this soft in Fog Lake City.

Soon, two teenagers appear in the backyard, one boy with a hat facing backward and one girl with bright purple hair. They look really similar for some reason.

"Ah! The twins have arrived!" says Jeremy, walking over to his siblings. He messes up the girl's hair and steals the boy's hat. Both complain and retaliate by smacking him, but not enough to hurt. I think the complaints and wails coming from Jeremy are just an exaggeration.

"Whose dog is this?" asks the girl, who I realise is probably Charlotte's younger sister, Quinn.

"That one's mine," says Charlotte, and I have a hard time finding out where she is until I see she's on the balcony above us, with a man who looks a lot like the young boy (who I think is Charlotte's younger brother Kyle) if he were about thirty years older flipping what I think are burgers on the grill. The smell makes my mouth water, and I realise how hungry I am.

"What's her name?" Kyle asks.

"Comet," replies Charlotte.

"Cool. Is dinner ready?"

Charlotte turns back towards her dad.

"Dad, is dinner ready?"

I hear a gruff response of 'almost', then Charlotte repeats the news to her brother. She listens for a bit to another faint voice somewhere in the distance, then:

"Mom wants us to help her set the table and cut the salad. Jer, bring Comet inside too and get her some water."

"On it! Come on, floof," says Jeremy. I've never been called a floof, but I like it.

Inside, everyone is working on various things, but all getting ready for the barbecue. Charlotte's dad is grilling, and now that I'm inside I can see that it's not just burgers, but corn and some sort of really big mushroom. Charlotte and her mom are making a salad, and the rest of the family is carrying trays of other dishes and empty plates outside onto a table I didn't notice when I was first playing with Jeremy in the backyard.

It makes me think of my own family, and while that in and of itself comes with a pang of pain in my heart, there's another feeling there now... pride. My family, even though they're not human and don't have barbecues, also work together and mess around with each other, and have the kind of love that is echoed throughout everything that we do, from helping each other with whatever we need to the casual conversation and communication that only comes with someone you truly love.

Scar and Brescia are great parents. The pups are so eager and so willing to be there for us doing whatever needs to be done. I… well, I suppose I'm just like the pups except I'm much older and can do much more. I bet if we were human, we'd be just like Charlotte's family.

Once everything is ready, we sit at the table in the backyard. I don't have my own chair, but I'm free to roam around the backyard after I've eaten the dog food that Charlotte gave me. Somehow it tastes different here than back home. As I explore, I notice some raised garden beds with big, juicy red tomatoes and beans longer than my ears. Charlotte's mom must be a gardener or something.

"Mom, can I give Comet some of my burger?" asks Quinn.

"I put some onion in those, better not," replies her mom. "Also, you slather that thing in mustard like nobody's business. There's raw beef in the fridge if you want to give her that."

"Oh yeah! I'll be back!" Quinn darts into the house, then yells from the balcony in about a minute. "I CAN'T FIND THE BEEF!"

"It's in the fridge, not the freezer, honey," says Quinn's dad.

"OH! GOT IT!" She runs back downstairs and approaches me, panting.

"Here. It doesn't seem fair that you get to just watch us eat all that lovely stuff, and you're stuck with the dog food. Come on, eat with us!"

I follow the smell of beef to a spot between Quinn and Charlotte, at the corner of the table. Quinn gives me what little beef there is left, and Charlotte slips me a bit of her big mushroom. I've never had mushrooms before. I wonder what it tastes like.

"Charlotte, honey, are you sure…" says her mom, head tilted a little bit in concern.

"Don't worry, I looked it up. Mushrooms are safe." Charlotte's mom nods and goes back to her food.

The mushroom actually tastes really good. Not as good as the beef, of course, but still tastes amazing. But none of that beats eggs. I wonder if we'll have eggs tomorrow. I love eggs.

After dinner, I spend a lot of time with the younger twins, playing with Frisbees and other dog toys, and getting a bunch of attention from the adults as well.

"So what's her story?" asks Charlotte's dad.

"She used to be a stray. Remember I told you about that fi… yeah," says Charlotte as her dad nods. My heart skips a beat. It's still a sensitive topic, even for humans.

"Can't believe you're only gone for a month to Fog Lake City, and you've already adopted a dog," says Jeremy. "But then again, it's not like it's completely unexpected of you," he continues.

The twins soon tire out of playing fetch and kneel down just to pet me. I end up lying down on the soft grass and clovers, fully content.

If you'd have told me a month ago that I'd be on a soft grassy field with a completely new group of people, surrounded by friendship and love and care, I would have scoffed in your face. It almost seems too perfect to be real now that I'm actually here. I love it here, but I don't think I'm meant to live here forever. Fog Lake City is my home, and always will be. The memories that I made there are still too dear to my heart. Of course there are some memories that I wish never happened, but that city raised me, along with Scar and Brescia, who are still there, and I could still see, even if the chances of that are really low.

Hope is stronger than you know, sometimes.

The next morning, everyone wakes up at their own time. I'm not used to being able to wake up at whatever point in time I want, so I end up feeling really sluggish when I do. But what eventually pulls me out of bed at the absurd hour of nine-thirty in the morning is the wafting smell of eggs and toast from the kitchen. I clamber out and see the morning sun coming through the window, bathing everything in a soft golden light. When I get to the kitchen, my food bowl has its regular kibble, but on top is one whole fried egg. My eyes widen. It's been so long since I've had an egg. My stomach rumbles as I lower my head to eat the egg. It tastes just how I remember, if not even better.

Charlotte is already sitting at the table, along with the rest of her family. I must be the last one awake. She's scrolling through her phone and sipping coffee delicately. It's probably still too hot.

"Mom, did you know about the market this weekend?" she asks. Her mom is sitting at the other end of the table, also sipping coffee.

"I did, and I thought maybe you'd like to bring Comet along too. You know the Hollises are going to be there selling their produce. They always have the best potatoes, I don't know how they do it."

"Sounds like a plan," says Charlotte. "What does everyone think?"

The family agrees, making various noises of approval. Some just nod.

Soon enough, we're all packed up and ready to go to the market. Charlotte's family car is pretty big, enough to fit all six family members *and* me. This time, I'm sitting in the back, between Charlotte and Quinn.

The drive to the market is slower and more casual than the drive here, but it still has the same fresh aroma in the air of herbs and other flora. I don't get to stick my head out of the window, but the windows are all rolled down, so the wind still gets to ruffle my fur. My tail wags, smacking the car seats on either side of me.

We find a parking spot and then get out of the car, strolling to the market slowly. It's amazing here. It's a long, blocked-off street with vendors selling everything from soap and candles to produce to makeup products and jewellery. The mix of smells — cinnamon and parsley and beeswax, for example — fill the air.

Everyone seems to know Charlotte's family. We stop at many different vendors' tents and stands. Charlotte buys a hand-knitted sweater for the coming fall and attempts to buy one for me, but then decides against it when she notices my unease. I've never been put in a sweater before, but I don't think I would enjoy it. Besides, my husky fur is thick enough.

Finally, we make it to the Hollis' produce cart. There's a fairly large open tent… roof… thing with tables on three sides, filled with carrots the size of my tail and squash that, if carved out, could make a dog bed for a small dog. Maybe even one of the pups. I wonder if maybe not, actually. The pups could have grown so much in the time I've been… away. A shame I missed that part of their life.

"Hey. Psst. You. Husky girl," says a voice from under the table in front of me. A Bernese Mountain Dog is laying under the table in the shade, panting from the heat. I lay down next to him.

"Hi? Who are you?" I ask.

"I'm the Hollis' family dog, my name is Pep. Pepper, really, but everyone always calls me Pep. Who are *you*, I must ask?"

"I'm Comet. My owner is Charlotte, as of a couple of weeks ago." Pep looks up at Charlotte for a couple of seconds, then looks back down at me.

"Welcome to Basil Hills, then, Comet," he says. "Are you liking it here?"

"I am," I reply. "Surprisingly." Pep raises an eyebrow at me.

"What do you mean 'surprisingly'?"

"It's... hard to explain."

"Try me." Pepper listens intently as I stammer through a simplified version of the past little while. He's a good listener, gasping at all the right parts and staying silent at the right ones as well. At the end, he smiles, and hesitates a bit before responding.

"You've gone through a lot, haven't you?" says Pep softly. I nod, pursing my lips.

"Yeah. Yeah, I have."

"Are you going to stay in Basil Hills, do you think?"

"No, I don't think so. I mean, first of all, Charlotte's going to college soon, and she has an apartment in Fog Lake City, so that's eliminating any chances right off the bat. And... look, call me sentimental or whatever, but my family is still back in Fog Lake City. I want to see them again. I still have hope."

"I see. Say, let me tell you something. I've been to many places. Many houses, many families, many cities, including the one you call home. In all of them, I've gotten attached to people and other dogs, and I've had to let them go. And they hurt every time."

"Really? Why would you make friends then if you know you're going to be hurt eventually? Isn't that just a recipe for disaster?"

"I'd rather live life surrounded by friends than a life of pain because I'm trying to potentially avoid it in the future. Does that make sense?"

Suddenly, everything clicks, and I'm rendered speechless for about a minute, my jaw opening and closing like a fish out of water as I try to wrap my head around this.

"You're… wow, you're right. But why are you telling me this?"

"Because you can still hope to see your family again, but changes in life are inevitable. Especially when you have an owner who doesn't know all that you've told me. Let's be real, Charlotte's lovely, but she doesn't speak dog. I'm not saying disconnect from your family. They were such a huge part of your life, and they will continue to be whether or not you see them. But you don't have to always be alone just because change happens. Don't be afraid to let people in, like you've done with Charlotte. Loving your family doesn't cancel out the possibility of loving others."

"Where did you get so wise?" I joke, but inside, I can't deny that it's like he's taken all my worst fears and my bad habits, laid them out in front of me, explained why I have them, exposed me and comforted me at the same time.

"Experience, I suppose. Just know that you are not alone in this world anymore."

You are not alone in this world anymore. I've never resonated so much with words of comfort and advice. I'm not alone anymore. I don't have to be.

"I needed that, Pep. Thank you."

"No problem, Comet. Always glad to help out."

"Come on, Comet, we're heading out to get lunch now," says Charlotte, pulling lightly on my leash while holding a paper bag of fresh veggies. "I see you've already met Pep."

"I might never see you again, Pep," I say as Charlotte lightly tugs on my leash to get me to stand up.

"And maybe you will, and whatever happens, you'll be okay. You will be, right?"

I pause.

"Yeah, I'll be okay."

"Good. I'll catch you later, whenever that may be."

"Bye!"

I walk beside Charlotte to a park, where we all have a picnic lunch. The twins take turns throwing a thick red rope across the field for me to chase. I can't believe just how much I've been robbed of the joy that comes from chasing a flying red rope.

That evening, after dinner, Charlotte and I get ready to leave.

"When will you be back?" asks her mom.

"Maybe I'll come around sometime in mid-October? I wanna get used to college life for a bit."

"Alright, sounds good, you just call us." Then Charlotte's mom does something completely unexpected. She kneels down beside me and pets me slowly, looking into my eyes.

"Comet's a lovely dog. You've picked well. I may have already said that before, but it doesn't matter because it's true." Then she addresses me directly.

"You're part of our family now, Comet, whatever family or friends you had before, you're one of us too. You're always welcome here."

One of us. Always welcome. I'm not alone anymore.

"That's good to hear, Mom," says Charlotte with a grin. "I'm sure Comet's glad to hear it, too."

Am I ever.

We say our goodbyes and climb into the car. Charlotte opens the window and I get my last scent of Basil Hills air for the time being. And I realise that I have two homes now. Two families, two sets of friends. And as much as I loved it in Basil Hills, I can't wait to see Fog Lake City again, and I find myself excited to see the types of adventures my life will bring me now too.

Charlotte rests her hand on my back and I fall asleep to the sound of soft rock music from the radio and the car engine whirring.

We get back to Fog Lake City and Charlotte pulls up in her apartment complex driveway. She nudges me awake, and I yawn drowsily before plodding upstairs slowly behind Charlotte, carrying her bounty that she brought over from Basil Hills. She sets her bags down on the ground and unlocks the door.

"Welcome home, Comet," she says, and I'm brought back to the first time that she said that, the first time I was in this apartment.

This time, it actually *does* feel like home.

Chapter 18: Reunion

Life will never be perfect. But Charlotte and I both try our best to work through any problems we may encounter. We're a team now. A family, of sorts.

As the summer days get colder and the breezes go from warm and refreshing to a slightly crisper chill, Charlotte decides to take me to the dog park. She thinks that it'd be better for me to be out and about among other dogs for a little bit, especially when the weather isn't as hot.

She brings a tennis ball and a weird contraption that allows her to throw the ball much farther than I think she could do on her own. We play fetch for a little while, then she sits down on a bench to read so that I can go, be free and meet other dogs. Someone else's owner is okay with throwing a rather large ball to more dogs than just their own, so I decide to join in the game. I'm not the greatest at it, but it's fun nonetheless.

At one point, when I'm not looking at the path in front of me, I end up colliding with another dog. This one is skinnier, and a dark grey colour. I run smack-dab into her side, knocking both of us over.

"Hey, watch where you're going, silly…" The voice. A very recognisable voice. I don't dare believe it. "Comet???"

"Maisie?" I look up into the face of one of my bestest friends in the whole wide world.

"COMET!" she yells, and gives me a big hug in the way only dogs can. "I knew it, I knew it, I *knew it*! I knew we'd see each other again!" I can barely speak. I can't believe that Maisie's actually here, in person, talking to me.

"Is it really you?" I ask.

"In the *flesh*! Oh, my goodness, how have you been? How has life been treating you, I see you have an owner now, tell me *everything*!" she gushes, and it's as if electricity and sugar syrup run through her veins instead of blood by the way she talks so fast.

I grin. Her energy is contagious.

"Have I got a *story* to tell you, my goodness," I start. I tell her *everything*. I forget to be sad as I tell certain stories and events because it's *Maisie*, and I'm so lucky and so extraordinarily happy to see her.

"So when the pups and all got adopted, right, of course I was like, super sad, but Willa — you know who… yeah, you know her — she was doing her best to support me, and we got to be kind of friends, but at first, I *totally* didn't want her to be…"

Maisie's a great listener, and her almost over-the-top reactions and cries of 'oh no' and 'wow' and 'oh my goodness' make me even more animated as I tell the story. By the end of it, we're both grinning so hard our jaws hurt.

"But enough about me, surely your story is the real deal!" I exclaim, laying on my back on the grass beside Maisie.

"So my owner's name is Blair, she has a boyfriend, but they don't live together, and Blair is *such* a fun person! She likes to go out with her friends, and sometimes they bring me along, and they dress me up in these cute different collars, almost like they're the dog equivalent of pretty dresses, and Comet, when I tell you those collars are some of the prettiest things I've ever had on!" she cries. Right now, she has on a simple one, but then again, if you're bringing your dog to the dog park, you probably don't want some sophisticated pretty jewelled collar.

"Blair is also wicked smart, she's a pharmacist so she works full-time but when she has her weekends she likes to go all out! She also has a *great* taste in movies! We watch movies together whenever she has a free evening, and she has this cute little pillow that's completely mine, and she treats me *so spoiled*! We're going to have such a fun-filled time together!" Maisie's voice keeps getting more and more high-pitched as she praises her new owner. I wonder if I'll meet her at some point.

"Do you want to meet her?" asks Maisie.

"You read my mind. Where is she?" Maisie cranes her neck and looks around. "I can't... oh! There!" Blair, Maisie's owner, looks up from her phone as she sits on a bench and waves at us. She's wearing a dress, and this one isn't as short as when she came in to adopt Maisie, but still very cute. She knows how to dress, that's for sure. Blair runs over and lovingly strokes Maisie's head.

"You've made a friend, Rosie! Hi, Rosie's friend!" I bark happily and Blair moves her hand as if to pet me, then stops. I'm confused and disappointed until she explains: "I haven't asked your owner yet if I can pet you, better not." Charlotte notices us, walks over and says hi to Blair and Maisie.

"Hey, I know you," says Blair. "You're Jeremy's younger sister! He was in that one biology class with me in high school, remember?"

"Yeah," says Charlotte. "He's back in Basil Hills, in case you were wondering, I'm just here for college. I might stay, though, but that's a decision for Charlotte-in-four-years."

"That's good! Hey, can I pet your dog, by the way?"

"Yeah, this is Comet. She's friendly, aren't you Comet, love?"

My tail wags as Blair kneels down to pet me.

"Thanks, Charlotte," says Blair. "Well, I'll let the dogs play, it was nice to see you!"

"Nice to see you too," says Charlotte, and the two part ways to their own separate benches.

"I thought I recognized your voices," says another, very familiar voice from behind us. Maisie and I whirl around to face the sound and at first, we don't see the dog who was talking to us.

"Down here, stupids," says the voice affectionately.

"M!" Maisie and I yell at the same time.

"No wonder we didn't see you," says Maisie. "You're so short."

M sticks her tongue out at us playfully. "It's not my fault I was born a toy poodle."

"M, how have *you* been?" I ask. "How are the kids, how's the house?"

"You ask like they're *my* kids, and *my* house," laughs M. "But they're great! They're so gentle, and so sweet! Tantrums happen almost once every few days, but then I can just go to the backyard since they have a doggy flap for me, and then I don't have to deal with it!" Maisie and I start laughing, and M joins in soon enough. Maisie and I interrupt each other as we both try to explain our stories over the last month or so, and somehow M seems to get the gist of what we're both saying. I suppose living with toddlers will give you the ability to pay attention to multiple things at once.

"This is a dream, honestly," says M. "I didn't think I'd ever see you guys again, but now that you're here, this is *so cool*!"

"Me too!" squeals Maisie. "Oh, the opportunities we have now!"

Images flash through my mind of meeting up with M and Maisie years in the future. Seeing the kids in M's family all grown up and playing fetch with us. Maisie's owner could maybe be married. Charlotte would be there, but now graduated and a little older.

I don't think my grin has faded since the beginning of this whole meetup, and either my jaw will hurt for a while or it'll be stuck that way. Whatever the case, it'll be worth it. My friends are here, and I'm not alone. Pepper's face appears in my mind and winks. I wink right back.

"What was that wink for?" Maisie asks.

"Nothing," I reply with a laugh. "You guys wanna play tug of war? Charlotte brought a rope, I think."

"You'll win, that's for sure," says M, "But I'm down anyway."

I walk over to Charlotte, and she digs out the rope from her bag and throws it out into the field. Maisie and I lock eyes, grab one end each, and tug as hard as we can. Maisie's grown stronger since the shelter, that's for sure, and M's commentary isn't helping my case much.

"Maisie's almost got it, she's almost, no it's Comet's, and now Mai... nope, Comet's got it, but wait... and now..."

Finally, with one hard tug, I pull and grab the rope all to my side, causing me to fall head over heels. Maisie giggles as I scramble to get back to my feet.

"I won," I announce.

"Good for you," replies Maisie. "Good game."

Maisie, M, and I decide to walk around the park together, reminiscing about all sorts of things while also talking about the new stuff in our life. There's a big collection of trees and bushes in the middle of the dog park field, and once we get around it, I notice four dogs running off together, collarless, young and thin. I wonder what they're up to.

But then I look at where they were running *from*, and I see two dogs that I think I could recognise anywhere. I could be gone from them for years, and could be losing my memory, and would still know these dogs. I stop short.

"Comet, what's wrong? You okay?" asks Maisie.

"I'm better than okay," I say with a tight voice. "I'm sorry, I gotta…" I take off running at full speed. "MOM! DAD! BRESCIA, SCAR, IT'S ME! I FINALLY FOUND YOU!"

Their faces turn, confused, and then their eyes widen. Scar's eyes shine in the early autumn light, and Brescia leans against him, moved, her eyes widening. I barrel into the two of them, emotions too overwhelming to say anything else.

"Oh my… Comet, my beautiful, beautiful daughter, it's you…" breathes Scar into my fur, and it's like I'm a pup again, and all that matters is my new mom and dad, and I'm safe and home.

"I missed you," I choke out. "I missed you so, so much."

Maisie and M have now approached us, but they stand a comfortable distance away, watching us. I think they understand just how important this reunion is.

"How have you been, Comet, love?" asks Brescia. "Stay there, I want to just look at you for a second." Brescia steps back and looks me up and down. Then she sighs, her bottom lip trembling slightly.

"You've grown. Not much, but you've definitely grown. And your fur is shinier and thicker, have you noticed?"

I haven't, but I'm glad to hear it. I shake my head and then approach Brescia and Scar to hug them again. Feeling their warm fur against mine is just as comforting, if not more, than it always has been.

We share our stories, crying as we speak, laughing through it all, between moments of just hugging each other with no thoughts, just pure love for each other.

Eventually, M and Maisie appear in the mix, telling their tales and getting hugs from Scar and Brescia as well.

I think this is the best day all year. No, not all year, maybe my whole life.

"COMET! COMET, COMET, COMET!" yells a young female voice. I don't even have time to register who it is before a small bundle of fluff and energy runs into me, knocking me over and licking my face so much I can't even open my mouth to laugh without either getting stepped on, licked, or getting fur in my face.

"COMET, DO YOU REMEMBER ME?"

"Of course, I do, Ellie, how could I — ack — forget?"

"Ellie, darling, get off your sister," says Scar. Ellie jumps off and bounces on the spot, excited to see me, as I get up and dust myself off. Dusty and Tina follow suit and almost knock me down, but don't at the last second.

"Dusty, you're so big now! How did you get so big?"

"I *grew*!" he announces.

"I can see that," I say with a smile. "How are all your guys' owners, tell me everything!"

Immediately I realise my mistake as the pups begin talking all over one another, voices getting louder and louder to get me to hear their story.

"…pool!!…"

"…so nice!! And gentle!!!…"

"…Comet, you wouldn't *believe*…"

"I'm so happy for you guys, honestly," I tell them.

"What about you?" says Dusty. "What happened to you when we were gone?"

I give them a very watered-down version of what happened to paint everything in a good light for the pups, and I leave out key details where sugarcoating isn't possible. The key details that I leave out, though, are told by M and Maisie in a very teasing voice.

"And then she *tore up the walls*! Classic."

"And it was all *black* and *burnt* and…"

The pups find Maisie's and M's little comments hilarious.

"What's all the fuss about now?" asks a quieter, deeper voice behind Scar and Brescia. I gasp, then sigh as I realise who this gentleman is.

"Oh, Darrell!" I cry. "I'm so glad to see you! How are you?"

"I'm doing perfectly fine, Comet darling," he says. "I heard your story, no need to recount, and I just wanna say I'm happy for you. You got a good life ahead of you." My smile wavers. Darrell is such a sweetheart.

"Did you get to do your 'relaxing'?" I ask with a cheeky grin. Darrell returns my grin with sparkling eyes.

"Did I *ever*," he says, sighing on the last word. "I love my owner, my goodness. He's such a great man. I would be happy with him for the rest of my life."

"You lucked out, Darrell. I'm glad," I say. "Come, join us." We all make room for Darrell and organise ourselves in a circle.

I look around at our group. Though our lives have all changed, most of us are the same underneath it all. You can tell that our experiences over the last little while have changed us. But I think, in the end, it's for the better.

We stand in silence for a little bit, just absorbing all the good energy, the only feeling being a deep sense of love and affection for every dog in our little circle.

"Group hug?" suggests Tina, and we all unanimously agree, approaching each other for a big doggy group hug. It's the most comforting thing I've felt in a while.

"I love you all. So, so, *so* much." I say, my voice a little strained. I might start crying again, but if I do, I know it will be out of love and of joy to be around these dogs that I care so ridiculously much about.

"Me too," echoes throughout the circle.

We break out of our hug, and I turn to my mom and dad.

"Who were those four dogs you were talking to?" I ask. "I don't recognise them." Scar and Brescia look at each other for a quick second before responding.

"Just because we're adopted, sweetheart, doesn't mean that the problem of stray dogs is over," Brescia begins. I nod in understanding.

"Pebble, Austin, Harley, and Rhea are four of the many strays in our city. We saw them and wanted to help them. We told them about the Den, and who we are, and encouraged them, told them that they will always be able to find help if they need it. Especially since many of the stray dogs in our city know *of* us, if they don't necessarily know us," says Scar. "I hope... no, I think they'll be okay. They're smart dogs."

"Did you hear they're taking the Den down? They're going to get rid of the eyesore that it is now," I say.

"Unfortunately, yes, I've heard that," says Brescia. "It's with a heavy heart that we have to acknowledge this, but the Den... at least, *our* Den... is a thing of the past now."

"It doesn't have to be," says Scar. "The house, sure, is gone. But the Den is more than the house. Brescia has been our leader even when we weren't living in the Den. We are all still family even with the fact that the Den is gone, and we'll end up going our separate ways after this. The physical Den is indeed in the past, but we are still here, and while we live, the Den lives on as well."

"Long live the Den," says M softly. There are a few seconds of silence.

"I don't want this to end," I say, a lump in my throat. "I don't know when we'll ever see each other again after this."

"We said that at the shelter, and look at us now," says Brescia. "There's still hope. There's always hope."

"Yeah, you're right," I say.

"And even if we don't... you'll be okay. We all will be," says Scar. "Right?"

Everyone starts nodding. We look like bobbleheads. As I look into the faces of all gathered here, there is no feeling I feel more than fierce love for every single one of them. I'll love them through my memories, and I'll love them when I bump into them, and I'll love them forever until I die. No matter where I live, and no matter where we are in life, and no matter who else I meet, nobody will ever matter more to me than these amazing and lovely dogs that I've had the absolute pleasure to have in my life.

Scar. My father. The first one to find me. Tough, but with a soft side.

Brescia. My mother. My role model. A charismatic leader, who cares for everyone and anyone she can, even more than herself, sometimes.

Maisie and M. Some of my best friends. They're always there for me, and I know I will always be there for them when they need me.

Ellie, Dusty, and Tina, my siblings. The energetic one; the quiet, gentle one; and the mature, careful one. All different, all dogs I am ridiculously proud of and love to no end.

Darrell. My friend, the amazing Uncle Darrell to the pups, peaceful and loving.

And while she is not with us now, we cannot forget Trey, another one of my best friends, my voice of reason, the playful, enthusiastic, fiercely protective dog that she was.

These dogs raised me. And while I will miss them when we're apart, I know that we are all in safe places now, and this is *not* the end. We *will* see each other again. And as the circle breaks, and we decide to play together while we still can in this city we call home, I realise that Scar's right, as usual.

We'll be okay. No matter what.

ACKNOWLEDGEMENTS

I can't believe that I have the privilege of being able to publish my second novel at seventeen years old. I'm honoured and also super proud of myself. But "Scattered" wouldn't be the book it is now without the help of so many important people.

I want to first and foremost thank everyone at Sulis International Press and Riversong Books: notably my editor, Neela Tudurí-Kłepfisch, for all the hard work you do to turn my manuscript into a proper book that people can read and enjoy.

I want to thank my parents for their undying support in me and my writing. I want to thank my mom for being my creative outlet and listening to my many ideas, and being the first one to read the roughest drafts of anything I write. And I want to thank my dad, who is always there to support me in any way he can.

I want to thank my beta readers, Grace and Elena, for looking over "Scattered" from the perspective of a reader and helping me find the good, the sad, and the filler from my rough draft. Your advice was incredibly useful and I hope you enjoy the final product knowing you had a hand in making it as perfect as it could be.

Every once in a while, I remember thirteen-year-old me in quarantine with too much time on her hands and a dream. I think she'd like to know that our dream came true.

So thank you to everyone who's supported me and been following me as I live out this childhood dream of mine. Here's to making many more wonderful stories.

ABOUT THE AUTHOR

If you feel generous and have a couple of minutes, please leave a review. It makes a huge difference to the author. Thank you in advance.

Catherine Khaperska is from Halifax, Nova Scotia, Canada. *Scarred* is her debut novel, and *Scattered* is its sequel, set about two and a half years later. Along with novels, she writes short stories, poetry, and enjoys dabbling in other forms of creative writing as well. Besides writing, Catherine enjoys gymnastics, dance, and playing her clarinet. As well, she is an avid knitter and crocheter, and she likes to spend time with her friends, family, and two lovely cats: Tiger and Luna.

Visit the author's website at
www.catherinekhaperska.ca

Follow the author on social media:
Instagram: www.instagram.com/catherinekwrites/

About the Publisher

Sulis International Press publishes select fiction and nonfiction in a variety of genres under four imprints:

- Riversong Books (fiction)

- Sulis Press (general nonfiction)

- Keledei Publications (spirituality)

- Sulis Academic Press (academic works)

For more, visit the website at
https://sulisinternational.com

Subscribe to the newsletter at
https://sulisinternational.com/subscribe/

Follow on social media
https://www.facebook.com/SulisInternational
https://twitter.com/Sulis_Intl
https://www.pinterest.com/Sulis_Intl/
https://www.instagram.com/sulis_international/